NAVAJO CANYON

NAVAJO CANYON

Tom W. Blackburn

THORNDIKE
CHIVERS

This Large Print edition is published by Thorndike Press®, Waterville, Maine USA and by BBC Audiobooks, Ltd, Bath, England.

Published in 2004 in the U.S. by arrangement with Golden West Literary Agency.

Published in 2004 in the U.K. by arrangement with Golden West Literary Agency.

U.S. Hardcover 0-7862-6462-4 (Western)
U.K. Hardcover 0-7540-9691-2 (Chivers Large Print)
U.K. Softcover 0-7540-6951-6 (Camden Large Print)

The text of this Large Print edition is unabridged.
Other aspects of the book may vary from the original edition.

Set in 16 pt. Plantin by Minnie B. Raven.

Printed in the United States on permanent paper.

===

British Library Cataloguing-in-Publication Data available

===

Library of Congress Cataloging-in-Publication Data

Blackburn, Thomas Wakefield.
 Navajo Canyon / by Tom W. Blackburn.
  p. cm.
 ISBN 0-7862-6462-4 (lg. print : hc : alk. paper)
 1. Navajo Indians — Fiction. 2. Large type books.
I. Title.
PS3552.L3422N385 2004
 813'.54—dc22   2004044042

For RICHARD PENOYER,
Incomparable Companion
At Canyon De Chelly.

ONE

For a long time days are endless, the difference between one and the next slowly adding up the sum of a man's experience. Sun and storm, good hunting and bad, with youth a leavening; things for remembering. The first surprise that the smoke of a buffalo-chip fire should smell so curiously sweet. A blizzard in Two-go-tee Pass when Parvenu and two Indians, all within arm's reach, walked blindly over an unseen brink and there suddenly remained only the company of the wind.

A night in the company of Jim Bridger under Crowheart Butte when it seemed a good idea to be free with Old Gabe's whiskey and so much of it went into Shoshone bellies that history was made with the first Sun Dance offered a full moon.

Good things for remembering.

Then suddenly one morning there is frost in the beard and in the hair when there is none on the ground. Blankets are warmer than they should be an hour after sunup. Old hurts are stiff. So swiftly as this, youth is gone. It is not old age, for this comes slowly. But a divide has been passed. The trail leads on as always, but it climbs no more peaks. The steady time of life is at hand. To some it is welcome.

Lindquist pulled up, saddened by this thinking, more and more recurrent the season past. There had been sporadic rainfall since breakfast. It had muddied the trail, strangely rutted for a country so empty and rugged. Miserable country for travel, posing man-sized labor for even a company of veteran cavalrymen to gain twenty miles across it in a day.

Freshened by the rain, the air carried odors of juniper and bunch grass and wet red soil. And pervading these, the turpentine tang of jack pine. Lindquist eyed the timber about him with a plainsman's appreciative eye for standing wood, but nothing else pleased him. He was saddlegalled, wet, and chilled by bursts of rain, and timber had no business growing in the middle of the biggest desert God had ever made. To top it all, there had been no sign of the fleeing Navajo for days — and the Army of the United States was paying him what could be regarded as good money to find such sign.

A hail sounded from Lindquist's left, toward a scab of corroded red sandstone which slanted up from the timber crowning the mesa and raised a dike across the arroyo he had been following. He swore and reluctantly reined his horse toward the sound. Young Grayson was probably a good officer. The troopers seemed to like him. But his confounded enthusiasm was exasperating. A man who could find anything in this whole country west of Santa Fe to get excited about was crazy, and Grayson had consistently been excited about everything out here from ticks to thunder.

As Lindquist reached the slant of the sandstone dike, Grayson came clattering back along it with little regard for the well-being of the good Army horse he rode and delightedly holding some new discovery up in his hand.

"Hey, Rick!" he shouted. "Lookee here!"

Lindquist looked. Grayson seemed to be holding up a pair of very small, very beautifully made Spanish boots, obviously but lately parted from their owner. This was impossible, but it was incontestably so. The polish on the soft leather was yet bright. It made as little sense as the sudden and complete disappearance of the Navajo revolutionists the detachment had been trailing all the way from the valley of the

9

Rio Grande del Norte. Lindquist was in no mood to speculate on probabilities. It was a lot easier to blame his own incredulity on Grayson's knack for turning up things which just didn't get anybody anyplace.

"Now listen, Steve —" he started in severely. He didn't get any farther.

"There's a spring and a kind of a pool down there," Grayson went on happily. "Horse was thirsty and so was I. Swung down to get a drink of water, and here's these little tootsie-covers sitting there as pretty as you please." He sucked in his breath before adding, a little too smugly, "Just waiting for me!"

Lindquist scowled. There was maybe no such thing as being too young for a commission in the Army of the West, but it was possible to be too damned young for this country.

"You dreamed them," he told Grayson firmly. "Gone from Santa Fe less than three weeks and already you're dreaming up women" — he squinted in analytic estimation at the non-existent boots in Grayson's hand — "foot size six."

Grayson was hurt. "Four and a half!" he corrected aggrievedly. "You find a pair of shoes like this and even you'd start dreaming, Rick. You aren't dead; you're just grouchy. Let Captain Pfieffer worry about where those blasted Navajo have holed up. This is important. Come on and help me find her tracks."

Lindquist's frown deepened. He didn't like looking at something in which he didn't believe. It put him in an awkward position. He had responsibilities. He was a civilian scout, attached to an Army command on recommendation of Kit Carson, himself pro tem Chief of Scouts. He was a familiar of and trader with the various Pueblo Indians of the upper Rio Grande as well as with most of the tribes of the Great Plains. He was very definitely a man who took no stock in a legend of Cinderella, particularly a Cinderella in a sere desert of tumbled red rock and sun-scorched uselessness which had been empty of life since the day time began.

He was distressed with Grayson. A thing like this made a man unhappy. Particularly if he was a man who had climbed out of his unreasonable twenties and had gotten a pretty sure grip on what made the world the way it was. He quit looking at the little Spanish boots in pure self-defense.

"I hate to tell you," he said to Grayson with what he felt was admirable kindness under the circumstances. "I really hate to

11

tell you. It'll probably make you feel like trading your saber in for a bigger one. But it looks like you've stumbled on the first sign of the Navajo we've had in days. Let's get back to the command and report. Those boots don't even look like they've been out overnight in the weather."

Grayson blinked. "Wait a minute!" he growled. "Are you saying these belong to a Navajo? Ha! If they do, you've been holding out on me and so has everybody else! The way I get it, the Navajo are a conniving lot, broken-toothed and murderous, and they probably smell like the devil. They talked the Rio Grande pueblos into a revolt. They killed Charlie Bent, governor of this spanking new Territory of New Mexico. And they disappeared into thin air. They aren't fit to live. *These* belong to a Navajo? Rick, you're an old man, but you've got more imagination than I have!"

Lindquist flinched a little. Grayson was going it a bit strong. He wasn't outright old. Just steadied down a bit was all. And Grayson had a lot to learn about the Navajo. They were undoubtedly in part all that he had said of them. Certainly there was no question some of the tribe was involved in the revolt which had cost Governor Bent and some other territorial officials their lives. But they were a strong race, intelligent and prideful, and there were women among them who could wear the tiny boots in Grayson's hand with easy grace.

"We catch those renegades we're after and they've got women with them and we're going to have to put blinders on you, Steve," he said. "Come on. We're doubling back. No use working out further ahead until the detachment's caught up. I'm wet to the underskin with that rain this morning, besides."

Grayson was a soldier. As they were scouting, Lindquist was in command, civilian or no. Grayson caressed the little boots and turned to stow them in his cantle bags. He froze in this position, looking back over the tail of his horse. His face sagged with astonishment. Catching this expression, Lindquist twisted around in the same direction.

At about twenty yards, in headband and clout and legginged moccasins, a jet-haired Navajo leaned against the pull of a stout bow. Sun winked from silver and turquoise studding the heavy leather bow guard which protected his left wrist. An arrow lay against the taut bowstring, its obsidian point mercilessly aimed at the center of

Grayson's broad-shouldered figure. Lindquist turned his head slightly and saw a similar figure in a cleft in the sandstone outcropping, motionless, bow bent, his own name on another arrow. He didn't have to look further. Where there were two Navajo there would be many. He briefly tasted again his scant morning's breakfast and swallowed hard against it. The rebels who had escaped the collapse of their uprising against the government at Taos and Santa Fe — the desert nation Kit Carson had been ordered to capture en masse and transport to reservation imprisonment at Bosque Redondo — had reappeared as suddenly as they had vanished.

Lindquist made a very guarded signal to his companion.

"Get rid of your gun, Steve. Drop it to the ground — carefully."

"Keep your guns, if you've a mind," a voice said irritably in Spanish. "I just want my boots!"

Lindquist felt the same empty expression he had earlier observed on Grayson's face overcome his own features. A sort of physical betrayal of inner stupefaction. Astride a silvered Spanish saddle on a small, sleek horse, bare feet thrust through hooded stirrups and hair yet wet as though from a swim, a girl glared over a small juniper bush which separated her from him. An extraordinarily beautiful and wholly unbelievable girl. Moreover, she seemed to be addressing herself to Eric Lindquist rather than to Lieutenant Grayson — in itself an unaccountable thing. Lindquist opened his mouth but was unable to proceed further. The girl shifted impatiently in her saddle.

"I want my boots!" she repeated, this time in English. Lindquist looked with some helplessness at Grayson.

"I wish you'd keep your dreams to yourself, Steve!" he complained.

"Do something —" Grayson breathed.

"One of you had better!" the girl said. She gestured toward the bowmen among the rocks. Lindquist drew in a slow breath. He waved one hand feebly.

"The boots —" he said.

Grayson looked at the boots in his hand as though he'd just discovered them, then dismounted so hurriedly he nearly spilled full length. He crossed to the girl and offered them up with what practically amounted to reverence. She took them and shoved her feet into them with a pair of quick, graceful movements which made the best of trim ankles beneath her flaring

15

skirts. She smiled at Grayson and nodded at Lindquist.

"Thank you," she said. And she started to rein her horse around. Lindquist belatedly remembered that Colonel Carson and the Army of the United States had imposed considerable trust in him on this expedition.

"Wait a minute, miss!" he called out, much more loudly than he intended. The girl looked questioningly back. "Where did those Indians come from?"

The girl raised her brows.

"What Indians?" she asked innocently.

Lindquist gestured impatiently toward the red rocks, but the bowmen were gone. There were only sandstone and juniper and the whispering of yellow jack pine on the higher slopes, just as there had been for days. Lindquist scowled at the apparition of feminine loveliness Grayson's enthusiasm for discovery had dreamed up.

"All right," he growled. "We're not looking and they're gone. So we're not smart. Now that's proved, call them back."

"What do I do, just whistle?" the girl inquired.

Grayson nodded. "Or ride back with us to the command. We've been trailing those red devils all the way down from Taos.

They've given us the slip in these mesas, but we're going to find them. Besides, I've got a hunch Captain Pfieffer will want to know what you're doing here and where you came from."

"Are you sure it isn't *you* who wants to ask questions about me?" the girl asked archly.

Lindquist considered the question unnecessarily personal. "Positive!" he said.

Grayson had stumbled back to his horse. He was sort of leaning against the feeding animal, holding himself up against surprise and the results of a calf-eyed inspection of the girl by an elbow hooked over the low pommel of his service saddle. He blinked both eyes.

"What's your name?" he asked.

The girl answered the question all right, but to Lindquist.

"Micaela Castaneda."

"Mine's Grayson. Lieutenant Steve Grayson. This over here is Rick Lindquist — Eric Lindquist."

The girl made a little bow from her saddle.

"Señores," she murmured in gracious acknowledgment, as though she was not at all deliberately withholding important information from a portion of the Army of

17

the United States. Lindquist scowled at Grayson in an attempt to shut him up and turned severely back to the girl.

"Look," he said. "We're soldiers. Understand? At least he is. We're trying to find some fugitive Indians. You know where some of them are. You're going to tell us where we can find them."

"Am I?" the girl asked. Her now booted heels thumped lightly against the barrel of her pony. The animal turned. She started away. Lindquist said a strong word under his breath, felt no better for it, and with admissible cowardice barked an order at Grayson.

"Stop her!"

Grayson swung up with a grin. It was obvious that in this moment he loved Rick Lindquist.

"Tell the captain I died gloriously in line of duty," he said.

The girl pulled up again. She frowned at Grayson, stopping him cold, and faced Lindquist.

"You and your men have come a long way. This isn't a hospitable country. Rest — water and food for your men and horses. I can offer you these. Tell your captain that if he will follow this arroyo I will make it possible for him to reach the Castaneda *estancia*. My father and I will expect you before dark."

Grayson smacked his lips quite audibly. Lindquist thought the sound distasteful. His scowl darkened.

"This is a military campaign, not a social tour!" he said stiffly. "We're looking for Indians, not hospitality!"

The girl shrugged. "You may find more Indians than you've bargained for if you and your men don't listen to what my father and I have to tell you!"

Her heels drummed against the ribs of her pony again and she rode away. Lindquist stared helplessly after her until the creak of Grayson's saddle drew his attention.

"Better follow her, I guess," he said with conviction.

Grayson chuckled. "Not only are you old before your time, Rick," he said, "but I do believe you've got the makings of a lecher! And determined to get a Navajo arrow in your back, besides!"

"All right," Lindquist agreed with more readiness than he was willing to admit. "We'll report back to the command. This is Pfieffer's headache now."

Grayson lifted a little in his stirrups. His eyes swept across a segment of the horizon in the direction in which the girl had disappeared. He breathed very deeply.

"Sure a wonderful country!" he said with feeling.

"For lizards!"

Lindquist jerked his horse around and pointed the animal across the broken mesa top toward distant ridges where Captain Pfieffer and the slow-moving, weary force under his command would be following the blazes Grayson and himself had left for them.

TWO

At first Captain Pfieffer thought it was all very funny. He told everybody so. The troopers thought it was funny too. Maybe because none of them had shaken down a good laugh in better than a week. They worked out variations of Lindquist's guarded report and circulated them freely. Most of the variations touched upon a sensitive portion of Lindquist's anatomy. He had never considered himself adept at romance and he fancied personal attack in the general hilarity. He was quite unhappy.

After all, it had not been he who discovered the little Spanish boots. He had been minding his own business — the search for Navajo sign. He had not dreamed up the barefooted girl. Was he going to put his mind to such a project, he'd have turned out a tall, willowy, dignified woman with an appreciation of a military man's problems — not a small, explosively dark-headed and slightly too curvaceous product of another man's imagination. But it was impossible to get a thought like this across to a practical and hardheaded man like Captain Pfieffer.

In the end Lindquist felt completely cornered. He felt quite hostile toward Steve Grayson for creating the whole situation. And he felt obliged to take immediate steps to clear himself. He was about as firm with Captain Pfieffer as his position as civilian scout permitted him to be.

"I will be obliged to make a report to the Chief of Scouts," he told the officer.

Pfieffer seemed to think this added additional humor to something already very funny.

"I'd give a month's pay to see Carson's face when he reads it — particularly if you'll let some of the boys give you a hand in putting it together, Lindquist."

Lindquist stiffened. "My report to Colonel Carson will state we made contact with the Navajo on this date, Captain. If you force me to add that the detachment commander did not see fit to act upon my advice, I won't hesitate to do so!"

Pfieffer's amusement vanished. He took Lindquist's statement in very bad grace, indicating that by and large he wasn't overly fond of civilian scouts in any event.

"I'm not in the habit of jeopardizing a command on the basis of hallucinations, regardless of whose they are. You and

Lieutenant Grayson report water in the arroyo you're talking about. That's all that interests me. We'll arrive there tomorrow forenoon."

"This girl and her father expect us by sundown," Lindquist repeated stubbornly. "That's what she said."

"You mentioned that," Pfieffer said shortly. "You have my answer. I'm detailing you back to advance scouting. When you can lead me to a Navajo encampment I'll consider leaving the open ground of this mesa top, but not before. Meanwhile, you can include anything that suits your rather active fancy in your report to Colonel Carson, so long as you don't ask me to act upon it!"

Lindquist considered a somewhat unmilitary reply but safely stifled it. Grayson pushed eagerly forward.

"Sir, I request permission to accompany Lindquist on this new patrol."

"You'll remain with the command," Pfieffer snapped. "Think I want to see the dependability of a good officer ruined? Besides, I want to know what our scout can turn up this time on his own. Be a pity to clutter up a genius like that with the company of a soldier!"

Pfieffer swung away before Grayson

could protest or Lindquist could lay hand to phrases even partially expressive of the heat in him. Grayson grabbed his arm appealingly.

"Look, Rick, we're friends —"

"We were," Lindquist said flatly.

"Quit grousing!" Grayson pleaded. "Why should I open my mouth? No use in Pfieffer thinking we're both liars. Look, now, be a good fellow. Tell her I tried to come along but got ordered to stay with the troop."

Lindquist tried very hard to be patient.

"Get this straight, Steve," he said slowly. "I'm going out hunting Indians. If I ever see that girl again it'll be because I've been shot from my saddle, both legs are broken, and I'm lying at the bottom of a pothole I can't crawl out of! Now get busy and try to square this with Pfieffer. You've got to convince him we did at least see two Navajo this afternoon. If you don't, he's apt to run the detachment into something it isn't braced for!"

Grayson stared at Lindquist in narrow appraisal.

"I wouldn't put it past you to be lying now, Rick," he said accusingly. "You try to pick yourself an ace out of the deck with that girl while I'm tied up here and

I'll never forgive you."

Lindquist had never murdered a man. He considered murder for a moment now — preferably by strangulation. It seemed a little too impractical, however, and he turned on his heel, leading his horse down to the remount group for replacement with a fresh animal.

This was a country of incredible twilights. Alone with the country as he had been so often alone with it most of his life, Lindquist felt his inner turmoil begin to ease. Something in the clean arid air here — perhaps its very cleanness and dryness — gave it a curious luminosity, so that long after the sun was down, strong light continued. At this time of day the red sandstone of the country rock ran a gamut of changing shades which set shadows at play so that where there had seemed a mountain now appeared a gorge, and stone escarpments which had seemed sheer and flawless were marked with great rents and dark, gaping passages. And all of it continued to change from one moment to the next so that there were no clear landmarks by which a man could operate.

Lindquist had worked down the arroyo at the head of which Grayson and he had encountered the two Navajo bowmen. He had found the pool beside which Grayson had found Micaela Castaneda's boots. He was perhaps half a dozen miles beyond this when he halted, faced with the end of twilight and the fall of full dark. With this came the realization he was no longer on the relatively unbroken top of the mesa but deep in a series of breaks which restricted vision and confused direction and that he was lost. Not wholly so, of course. He just wasn't sure where he was.

A man got a reputation as a frontiersman and a scout for reporting the astonishing with brevity and for a knack at finding his way about in unfamiliar country as well as in his own bailiwick. The way he saw it, Lindquist had raised the devil with his reputation today all the way around.

Afternoon heat still held in the drainage fissure he followed. But a faint puff of wind brought a breath of cooler air, promising somewhat lower ground ahead. A freshet-cut barranca carved into the soft stone, perhaps, and maybe even the water he would need for his horse and himself to night it here in comfort. He followed this cooler stream of air, hunched disgruntled in his saddle and growling to himself. He twisted a little to one side, watching the rim of the fissure for a likely deadfall from which to break firewood. As a result of this position he was nearly thrown when his horse made a sudden stop.

Instinct caught Lindquist. He threw his weight into his stirrups and jerked his attention ahead. One hand reached almost hopefully for his gun. The gesture was as useless as it was automatic. No man carried a weapon equal to what lay before him. Perhaps a quarter of a mile away, its true distance an eerily difficult thing to estimate in the deepening darkness, an immense wall of stone raised itself from a level, sandy bed for a breathtaking thousand feet of vertical cliff face which supported a piñon-crested rim at about the level of his eyes.

Between him and this huge wall swam a dark void which ended at the front feet of his horse. Lindquist swallowed slowly and with difficulty, blinking in an effort to reduce the effect to a more believable perspective. But the void remained and the opposite towering wall, and he realized his horse had stopped on the lip of a deep, sand-floored canyon as cavernous as the mesa across which he had been riding for a week was high. A spectacular knife cut of a canyon without the usual river at its bottom — a stupendous barrier cut through a country reported and mapped an uninterrupted mesa and therefore likely never before seen by a man of his own race.

He was dry, hungry, and in no mood to drink in the awesomeness of nature, but he made no move to turn his horse. He was sitting motionless when the animal stirred restlessly of its own accord and started across a slab of wind-exposed rock. A sandblasted piñon of unusual size, clinging to a touch of life only in a few straggling needle bunches, grew out of a crevice in the stone. A huge scar on its near side betrayed the regularity of an old blaze mark. Lindquist turned his head to peer more closely at this, and his horse tipped down from the slab of rock onto a narrow, hidden trail reaching across the broken upper fall of the near canyon wall.

Lindquist took up his reins, intending to back the animal, but a sound reached him from the depths below. A curiously believable sound, but so out of place in this vast emptiness that it seemed far louder than its actual faintness warranted. The yelping quarrel of a pack of Indian dogs dividing a supper. An unmistakable sound to a man who knew it. And with it came the smell of smoke on the air — the smoke of a cottonwood fire. He flicked his reins a little, and his horse moved more briskly down the trail across the face of the cliff.

A man could measure time by the arc a star traveled through a night sky. Or by the distance covered on a reliable horse. Or by the increase in night chill as minutes passed, if nothing else would do. But Lindquist found it impossible to determine how long he had been in making the descent of this canyon wall. Part of the trail was good, powdered to dust by the knife-hoof tread of sheep and stained by their droppings. Part of it was dangerous, laboriously hand-cut into the stone and overhanging empty space. The sky became a narrowing strip, confined by the rising walls of the canyon as he descended. And it was impossible to know if the increasing chill was because of the lateness of the hour or because of the stony depth of the chasm he was penetrating.

He felt the tremor of a shiver. He didn't know what caused it, which was, he realized, the same as being shaken by something he didn't understand. Familiarity with the mountains and the great spaces and the big things which lay west of the Missouri had bred a certain casualness in him, but it failed him now.

It was with almost relief that he heard a small sound near at hand. A familiar, identifiable sound which held nothing of eeriness — the ratcheting of a rifle hammer being drawn back to full cock. He reined his horse up and sat motionless, eyes probing the shadows about him. There was no movement.

"Lindquist," he said to the night. "Lindquist, of Colonel Carson's command."

There was a stir which echoed and re-echoed as a small sound often does in night stillness. But these were not true echoes. They were the sounds of many similar small movements being repeated. Lindquist shivered slightly again, realizing he was in the heart of an ambush which numbered perhaps a hundred rifles like the one he had heard being cocked.

Quick, light footfalls sounded among the rocks, approaching. A soft, familiar voice spoke rapidly in Spanish.

"It's all right, Chin-yi. Be sure there are no others."

A murmur of assent followed, and a moment later Micaela Castaneda appeared at Lindquist's stirrup.

"You're late," she said. She let down the hammer of the rifle she carried across her forearm. "I said sundown."

"Sorry," Lindquist said with considerable venom. "Had quite a welcome ready for the detachment, didn't you?"

The girl seemed unaware of his acidity.

"We're never sure of guests here," she answered. "We've learned to be careful in Canyon de Chelly."

"The Army's learned to be careful too," Lindquist said. "You can tell whoever's with you they don't need to wait. I'm alone."

The girl turned and spoke rapidly in Navajo, a curious run of singing syllables in which the rise and fall of inflection were almost oriental. Lindquist had heard no other dialect like it among the other pueblos. A boy whose brown torso merged with the night before he stepped back a pair of yards brought up a horse for the girl. She swung easily up and reined in beside Lindquist.

"Dinner will be cold."

"I said I was sorry."

"Yes. So nicely, too." The girl looked long at him and smiled a little. "I was disappointed at first. Now I believe I'm glad you came alone."

Lindquist looked meaningfully off into the night where the whispered movement of many men was fading into silence.

"So am I!" he said.

The girl frowned slightly. "It isn't that. It's just that maybe it will be easier to talk to one man instead of to many, after all."

"But you wouldn't know much about talking to men, would you?" Lindquist asked mockingly.

"Enough," the girl answered. "Perhaps not as much as you expect. That's something I can explain later."

"You can start any time," Lindquist said with feeling. "There's a lot to explain!"

The girl looked questioningly at him. He growled at her.

"So you think you're fooling? You tried to ambush a whole detachment of United States cavalry tonight — with the aid of a bunch of renegade Indian fugitives!"

"I didn't fail completely, did I? At least I got me one man!"

The girl laughed. Lindquist didn't care for her humor or the bland speculation with which she continued to survey him. It seemed almost as though he were something of clay she'd just taken from an oven, shaped by her own hand, and not too bad for a first effort. He continued to scowl, and her smile widened. But the curve of her lips didn't soften the bite of her next query.

"Are you coming with me or do I ask Chin-yi to have some of his men bring you along?"

Lindquist had a healthy respect for hostile Indians, particularly when he couldn't see them.

"I'll take my chances with you."

She kicked her horse lightly in the ribs. "You're a braver man than you realize." She laughed again.

Lindquist followed her on down the virtually invisible trail. There seemed little else he could do.

THREE

In a hundred yards more of descent they left the canyon wall at its base and cut out across the sandy floor he had seen much earlier from above. The sand was soft and cut by the hoofs of a thousand horses, but the canyon seemed entirely empty. Presently the girl pulled up and indicated the towering escarpment behind them. A bulging shoulder of rock stood boldly out into the starshine. Across it, apparently on a loop of the trail Lindquist had followed down from above, a silent, jogging file of Indians was visible. Hundreds of them, moving with the sureness of armed men.

"You understand now?" the girl asked softly. "You see why I wanted to talk to you? Sometimes it is wiser to talk than to hunt blindly, even when the hunters are soldiers of the United States Army."

Lindquist squinted calculatingly at the armed file above.

"Navajo?"

The girl nodded. "This is their home."

Lindquist considered the bland simplicity of this statement. The Navajo were

34

a known race of nomads, living chiefly on sheep and temporarily cultivated corn patches. Their beginnings were a mystery to men who had worked out the roots of virtually every other nation of the West. He doubted that the most learned experts on the Indian had ever thought of the Navajo as a nation, as having a home. Yet this girl seemed very certain. She gestured across the sandy floor of the canyon toward the opposite wall.

"It has been home to the Indians a very long time, this place," she added quietly. "Look —"

For a moment Lindquist saw nothing but the great, sheer walls which marked this place. Then he realized he had not tilted his gaze high enough. Three hundred feet above the canyon floor a huge, shallow cave was flaked back into the mother rock of the mesa. A large building stood in this recess. Not as large as the bigger of the two pueblos at Taos, perhaps, but far older, out of a forgotten time, and beautifully preserved. The upper story was stuccoed with a white gypsum of unusual luminosity, so that it stood out as though the moon shone for it alone.

There was no apparent means of communication between the floor of the canyon and the dead city above. Time had destroyed ladders. If there were handholds carved into the rock of the cliff face, they were invisible at this distance. The whole effect was of a mirage, a reflection out of antiquity. Life had indeed been lived a very long time here.

"White House," the girl said.

Her face was upturned to the ruin and the stars. Lindquist was aware a powerful force was stirring in her, softening her voice and her eyes. He thought he understood.

"The Navajo say it was built the Day-before-the-Beginning," she went on. She paused again, then turned to him with sudden fierceness. "Do you see now why your soldiers must not hunt here?"

Lindquist, caught in the curious spell of ancient things, started to nod. He caught himself in time and looked levelly at the girl.

"No," he said.

Her lips flattened into a straight line of startling grimness.

"You will!" she promised. "Come on. My father is waiting for us and he doesn't like to wait."

She lifted her horse into a lope across the soft, spraying footing of the canyon floor. Lindquist followed in her tracks until the sand kicked up by her horse stung his face. He tried to overtake her then, but for all its barrel build, her little pony could run like the wind. Or it understood the sand underfoot better than Lindquist's iron-shod cavalry mount.

The girl was a rod ahead of him when they reached a fence of thin cottonwood poles lashed with willow strips to piñon posts. They passed through an open gate in this and entered a compound flanked by a tiny, round sheep corral, a larger enclosure for horses, and a dozen or more hemispheric, clay-plastered Navajo hogans. Beyond these, where a bench rose safely above danger from flash floods on the floor of the canyon, sprawled a considerable house, low-roofed and stone-walled. From the windows of this glowed the hospitable light of good oil lamps. Lindquist pulled up.

To find such an establishment here was no less of a wonder than the looming silence of White House. And unlike the ancient ruin, this building had significance — military significance — the kind of thing Rick Lindquist drew good Army pay to find. He dismounted unhurriedly and dusted loose sand from his clothes with a slapping hand. When he straightened, the girl was at the entry of the house, holding the door open, waiting for him. He crossed to her.

"My house is yours," she said after the Spanish fashion. "Welcome to Estancia Castaneda."

Lindquist had not made a bow for a long time. He tried one now, stiff and awkward, and stepped into the house ahead of her.

A large room faced him. Its flooring was as red as the earth outside, huge flakes of shaling sandstone, set smoothly in mortar. A wide, squat fireplace dominated the far wall. It also was stone red in color. Floor and hearth showed surprising signs of age and much use, deeply worn with the scuffing of many boots. But they were scrupulously clean.

Furniture roughly fashioned of piñon and rawhide was comfortably scattered about the room. In the corner nearest the kitchen was a huge table surrounded by willow-work chairs. It was covered with a good cloth and set with a cooling dinner yet pervading the room with a smell good in Lindquist's nostrils. A deep chair near the fireplace held a very old man, fragile, white-headed, and hawk-nosed. A kind of terrible old man, since the helplessness of advanced age failed to hide completely an

38

immense strength and a driving dominance. The girl spoke to him.

"One of the *yanqui* soldiers, Father."

Apparently this was sufficient introduction. The old man's eyes dissected Lindquist with dispassionate thoroughness. Only when the inspection was complete did the eyes warm. The old man smiled a little.

"One of the two *yanquis* you saw this afternoon. Yes. This would be the older one. The — ah — handsome one."

The girl colored. Lindquist felt warm for the first time since sunset. Steve Grayson was a fine figure of a man, young enough and shrewd enough in a woman's ways to be charming. But apparently he had not made much of an impression on Micaela Castaneda. Lindquist tried to remember when a woman had last called him handsome and was shocked at the number of years which turned up. His mother had been dead a long time.

"The rest of the soldiers didn't come. Only" — the girl paused and surveyed Lindquist as though measuring him for his proper station — "only Major Lindquist."

"Just Lindquist," he said. "Eric Lindquist. Scout."

"Yes," she said gravely. "Rick, wasn't it?

39

This is my father, Pablo Castaneda."

Lindquist and the old man uttered the Spanish salutation at the same time.

"Señor —"

The old man sighed. It was a physical expression of a physical defeat. The deep breath of a weary man whose spirit drove him beyond the endurance of his body. His words were soft, deceptively so, but there was no deception in their meaning.

"It would have been better to have all the soldiers at once. But I knew we were to have bad luck when there was no sound of guns. Chief Juanito will be angry with us, Micaela."

"Let him be angry with some of his young men first!" the girl said with spirit. "It was their clumsiness which brought the soldiers here. Besides, the *yanqui* Army isn't in the canyon yet. Only one man. We may be able to do what is necessary with him."

She looked at the laden table.

"I'm hungry."

The old man rose from his chair. "But of course. And our guest —"

He smiled with complete friendliness at Lindquist and called out sharply. The door to the kitchen opened. Two startlingly large Navajo men entered. They had a prideful carriage and light walk Lindquist found disconcerting in household help. He was straightened out on this in a moment. The old man spoke swiftly in the Navajo tongue. The two Indians looked at Lindquist with a measuring, anticipatory pleasure. They started for him. He braced himself and stepped back a couple of paces. A thickly woven native rug skidded under his feet. Before he regained his balance, the two Navajo were upon him.

They were rougher than necessary inasmuch as Lindquist had long ago learned that appraisal of odds and submission to them were one method of avoiding needless mayhem. Resistance here seemed unwise and he offered none. They peeled his belt, gun, and knife from him and took his jacket for good measure. This last distressed him most. He had been on the trail for weeks and had for some time not seen fit to wash himself with much attention above his wristbands. This was in part because of scarcity of water on these mesas and in part a trail man's inclination to expend energy only upon essentials. His forearms were more bronzed than attributable to the sun because of the red earth powdering them to the elbow-length sleeves of his knit underjacket. And this garment all

41

too plainly betrayed the carelessness of the Spanish-American woman who had last laundered it for him at Taos.

"Friendly," the old man said in unruffled explanation when the Indians stepped back. "Completely friendly, you understand, señor. Merely cautious. We have not before had a *yanqui* soldier as our guest."

Lindquist scowled at his host and tried to rub some of the red dust from his forearms. He considered pointing out that Castaneda's daughter had twice been completely alone with him — when he was armed — without encountering difficulty. Cautiousness here, in view of this, seemed unnecessary. However, he said nothing of this.

"I'm not a soldier. But you'll get used to them if your Navajo friends keep on being hard to find. There are a lot of soldiers in the Army."

"Yes." The old man nodded. "But the whole Army isn't here. Just thirty men. I believe the count is accurate."

Lindquist nodded. It was completely accurate, to the man. There seemed no point in denying what was obviously already known as fact. Either Castaneda or the Navajo apparently had some able scouts of their own.

"And how many Navajo are in the canyon this season?" Castaneda asked his daughter.

"Four thousand. Four thousand regulars. I don't know how many more have come in from the mesas ahead of the soldiers."

"Four thousand, yes." Castaneda smiled. "These are very satisfactory odds, Señor Lindquist. Come, sit down. I think we should talk about how to save those thirty lives of yours — if possible."

Lindquist sat down. His chair was small and creaked alarmingly under his weight. The table was built for smaller men than himself. He felt uncomfortable, the more so because the old man kept his eyes on him with a friendly fixity which was far from reassuring.

The girl ate with relish, but he was aware that she was also watching him closely. He endured the strain for a little, but he had never been a particularly patient man, especially when dealing with something he knew must be faced sooner or later. Pushing back in his chair, he faced his host firmly.

"I didn't ask to come here. I didn't want to. Now I am here, I don't like it."

The old man waved his hand as though

he understood perfectly.

"There *is* an air about this canyon which is disturbing," he admitted. "Perhaps a feeling one intrudes upon a shrine of the ages. A temple of civilization hallowed by time. But it is a feeling one gets over as one comes to realize what Canyon de Chelly really is. Yes. As I say, one gets used to it."

"Those Navajo I saw tonight on that trail up on the canyon wall — they're from the Rio Grande Valley?"

The old man didn't seem to hear him. He nodded his head in reflective continuation of his own thoughts.

"I know de Chelly," he went on. "I should. I built this house. Over forty years ago. Micaela was born here. We own much land here, given to our family before I was born by a king who didn't even know this canyon existed. We've been permitted to keep the land because we've been from the beginning friends of those to whom it really belongs — the elders of the Council of the Navajo nation."

Lindquist had a curiosity about this man and his daughter — their beginnings and the reason they had been lost deep in these mesas — deep in an area even Spanish Santa Fe believed uninhabited by any of the old Southwestern race. But it was a personal curiosity. His business was official.

"Do these elders know a large party of their young men stirred up a revolt along the Rio Grande?" he demanded. "Do they know some of their people are murderers? Do they know there is a law out here now and these men must be punished?"

"There is nothing the Navajo elders do not know, señor," Castaneda answered quietly. "They are wise men."

"All right," Lindquist said. "Send them a message for me. Tell them the soldiers have been ordered to capture every Navajo on the mesas and escort the whole nation south to a reservation set aside for them — where they can be watched. Tell them they'll have to go. Tell them if they continue to hide or if they make a fight it will go hard for them at the reservation."

"This is what the soldiers intend?"

"My party has been ordered to attack, as against an open enemy, at the first sign of resistance. Get me an answer to take back to my captain."

The old man looked uncomfortably about him.

"Hardly a proper subject for the dinner table," he apologized. "I'm in a difficult position, señor. For many years the

Council has come to me for advice. It has listened to what I have to say. Can I tell four thousand of a prideful people to surrender to thirty whom they hate when it means they must leave de Chelly?"

"What you advise them is on your conscience," Lindquist said bluntly. "But I want my message delivered."

Pablo Castaneda shrugged with a wry smile.

"And I have a message from the Council also," he said. "Every *yanqui* who enters Canyon de Chelly will be destroyed."

Lindquist was aware of the effect this was expected to have upon him. Perverseness, a stubbornness, rather than any stiff-necked code of valor, made him ignore it with a dry ease.

"I'm a *yanqui*. A worse one than most. But you're feeding me in your house."

The old man nodded guiltily. "I am a very foolish man. I keep poor faith with my Indian friends. But there is a limit to my hospitality, Señor Lindquist. I must remember I have kept my lands by believing in most things as the elders of the Council believe."

Lindquist rose from the table, abandoning the meal while he was yet hungry.

"All right," he growled. "Then what do you do?"

"It's a matter of self-preservation," Pablo Castaneda said. "Surely you understand. I have little choice. My family has always done what was required to keep its land. Without land a man is nothing. And after me comes Micaela. I must think of her also."

For all his courtliness and quiet, the steel in Castaneda was apparent. These were not empty words. There was no question in Lindquist's mind that, had Captain Pfieffer ordered his command to follow up Micaela Castaneda's invitation to food and water at this *estancia*, the Navajo force stationed on the trail into the canyon would have set upon it and wiped it out to a man. For all the pleasantry at this table, the brevity of his own future seemed certain. Lindquist turned accusingly to the girl.

"You got me into this."

She widened her eyes at him.

"Not into the canyon. You came on your own horse, with no one leading you down the trail."

"All right. I'm going out the same way!"

Pablo Castaneda looked up in protest. "But we have not yet had wine!"

Lindquist glared at him, feeling the old man was laughing behind the opaqueness of his faded eyes. Swinging on his heel, he

47

took a long stride toward the door. He had the impression the old man raised his shoulders in a slight, mildly unhappy shrug behind him. He thought the girl started up out of her chair. But that which struck him came from neither of them. From an open window, perhaps. The blow robbed him of speech. It darkened the room. It shook all the rigidity from his knees, and the floor slanted swiftly up at him out of the darkness. As he fell, he knew what had happened.

Somewhere, from some angle, a sharp-eyed bowman had fired a bird-stick at him. A blunted arrow, carrying at its tip a carefully shaped head of rounded stone, larger than usual size, designed to stun but not to kill. An excellent weapon for game too prized to maim and especially effective against a stubborn and impatient man.

Lindquist had an instant of relief that enough consciousness remained to recognize this. In a place where many arrows with keen war-heads were available, he was fortunate a blunted point had been used on him. A dead man would have a devil of a time getting out of this canyon. One who was yet alive might have a chance — if he took what came and waited patiently for it. He slid on into an abyss of blackness as his body hit the floor.

FOUR

For a long time Lindquist listened to the blood pounding through his aching head. It had a peculiar irregularity which troubled him. Finally he stirred and sat up. The ache became immediately worse, but he discovered what had been troubling him about it. The pounding was not in his head at all, but in the air itself. He opened his eyes. He was dressed as he had been when he hit the floor in the Castaneda house. He was lying on a thick bed, the down for which must have cost a fortune in trade. He was in a bedroom of the *estancia*.

The pounding again drew his attention. He slid out of his knee boots and crossed to a small window. The sash was without hinges or conventional catches and was hung in place by little pivoted wooden cleats. He turned these and lifted the sash from its frame, standing it against the wall beside the opening. From the window he had an oblique view of the row of Navajo hogans he had earlier noticed as he rode in with Micaela. A small fire burned before the central one of these. A number of Indians were gathered about it, but with the exception of an old man who was urging a pounding rhythm from a small drum with remarkable skill, they seemed to be doing nothing.

Lindquist remained at the window for some time, letting the ache in his head subside and speculating as to whether or not all the Navajo immediately about the house were gathered around the fire at the hogans. He thought it was well past midnight, and the drum certainly meant a ceremonial of some sort, even if the inactivity of the Navajo about the fire belied this. It seemed worth the risk to see if they had forgotten the Castanedas' prisoner. Even if they had not completely forgotten him, Rick Lindquist had walked out of an Indian encampment before when his captors believed him secure. He turned back from the window for his boots.

Hanging on the foot of the bed were his belt and jacket. His knife had been removed from its sheath, but his gun was still in its place. He checked and found its loads had been drawn. He grinned as he pulled on the jacket and buckled on the belt. This little touch with the gun was undoubtedly the girl's work. It would take a woman to fail to realize that even an unloaded gun in the hands of a man accustomed to the weapon was still a very usable instrument. It would ease certain discomforts in him to make use of this obvious mistake. The Castaneda girl was so confoundedly sure of herself.

There were a few bad moments getting out through the window. It had not been fashioned for the convenient escape of a man as large as himself. Once outside, he edged carefully around the dim circle of light from the little fire at the hogans. The dogs inevitably about the domed huts worried him most. However, for some curious reason, they apparently failed to sense his movement or pick up his scent. He wondered if the drumming of the old Indian at the fire had dulled the perception of the animals. It seemed possible. The steady throbbing of the drum was an insistent thing, and Lindquist had to close his mind to it to prevent the sound from absorbing his own attention when he needed it elsewhere.

He reached the fence bounding the bench on which the Castaneda house and the Navajo hogans stood. Turning here to survey his back trail with precautionary care, he discovered that two dancers had joined the drummer at the fire. Young men, he thought, moving through a pattern of motion so intricate and unharried that Lindquist thought it might have been a ceremonial dance such as this which had earned the Navajo their general reputation as a lazy people.

He watched longer than he intended. There was considerable fascination in the remarkable precision of the slow-moving dancers. Their complete devotion to the rhythm of the old man's drum and the fact that only these two — not the entire group of the Navajo — were involved in the dance were indications this was a ceremonial of appeal to the uppermost gods. Beyond this, Lindquist could make no further identification. He had never seen an Indian dance to resemble this one.

Relieved that the Navajo about the house, at least, seemed sufficiently occupied, he slid carefully down from the bench to the floor of the canyon. His intention was to make a wide circle out across the canyon floor and double back along the wall behind him to the foot of the trail by which he had descended from the mesa crown. This would give him some opportunity to mislead pursuit, should his absence be discovered, and to approach the foot of the trail from an unexpected direction.

However, he realized he had made a mistake when he took his first step on the sandy canyon floor. The soft stuff was a page which would record his direction and strategy to any who might follow. The best he could do was trace the tracks of horses where he could, matching his prints to those of hoofs in an effort to hide them. It wasn't easy work. A horse did not stride like a tall man, and watching the ground underfoot so closely made walking difficult.

Minutes passed. The beat of the drum in his ears didn't recede. He looked behind him and found the Castaneda place shrunken to a pin point of light in the distance. He wondered if some trick echo among the standing walls of the canyon kept the drum sound at its constant pitch despite increasing distance. A few minutes later he discovered this was wrong. In angling across the canyon floor, he approached another small bench. Young cottonwood growth opened up here to reveal three more hogans in a close family group. Another small fire burned among them. And two more precise dancers circled with monotonous slowness before another grayed drummer. The sound of the ceremonial behind had been overlapped by that of the one ahead without a loss in the rhythm of the drums.

There were dogs here too. But as before, they seemed engrossed in the sound of the drums. Working cautiously back a little toward the center of the canyon, Lindquist passed the hogans without detection. There was a five-acre plot of corn — actually small-eared desert maize — thickly grown but no more than three feet high. A fence. Then a field which might have been in some unfamiliar kind of Spanish bean. Beyond this a knife-edge out-cropping narrowed the canyon to a width of a few yards. When he passed through this narrows, Lindquist was forced to halt again.

Stacked against the northern wall of the canyon and climbing upward, ledge to ledge, for hundreds of feet to a cavern halfway to the stars was another of the dead cities which seemed to be so much a part of Canyon de Chelly. Lindquist sat down on the sand where the overhang of the near canyon wall cast black shadow and sheltered him from starshine and chance visibility. He looked long at the empty, powdering buildings climbing the red stone of the opposite wall. The beat of the Navajo drums continued in his ears. And a peculiar feeling came over him. A feeling that tonight these drums were not talking to the higher gods but to a *yanqui* scout named Eric Lindquist. For a moment he almost understood their message. But before it could shape clearly in his mind he pulled himself together.

If the drums had anything of real value to say, it could be only a reminder that his life was valueless if he was caught and that Captain Pfieffer's force was apt to run into an enemy it couldn't handle unless he could get back to the command with a warning that the hiding place of all the Navajo had been found. He came reluctantly to his feet.

A quarter of a mile farther onward he worked past another group of hogans. There was again a small fire, a drummer, and the dancers. A dog here wheeled and came trotting half the distance out across the sand to him. Then suddenly the dog seemed to identify him as a familiar not worth further investigation and so trotted back to the fire. Lindquist scowled. The dogs troubled him. Nothing was as alert, troublesome, and noisy as an Indian dog. These in the canyon were acting most strangely.

Above the last hogans the canyon straightened out for a quarter of a mile or more into a kind of chute. Recurrent high waters had stripped out any benches of deposited silt here, so that the sandy floor extended from the base of one wall to the base of the other. Assured that he need not watch for more hogans in this section, since there was no high ground on which they could be built, Lindquist traveled more swiftly.

The horsemen who habitually traveled the canyon had showed considerable individuality in the course they took lower down. Their tracks had been widely scattered. Here, however, all seemed content to follow a deeply rutted trail close against the base of the south wall. Puzzled by this, Lindquist tilted his head up to discover that the wall was badly eroded and fell back for some distance, giving anyone approaching along this section of the south rim easier access than elsewhere to the very edge of the chasm. For this apparent reason the Navajo hugged the base of the wall in passage, protected from chance view from above by a bulging overhang.

The smooth sand in the center of the canyon floor was too tempting to pass up when it was certain most of it would be visible from the rim. Grayson, for instance, would not sit tight in camp when

Pfieffer's command hit the water in the arroyo up on the mesa. He'd head in the direction he'd seen the Castaneda girl take. Luck might bring him to such a break in the canyon rim as that above. Or Pfieffer might cool off sufficiently to reconsider his scout's report and do a little investigating. It was worth the chance.

Quitting the tracks of the horses, Lindquist walked out onto the unmarked sand. He walked about a four- or five-acre tract of this with apparent aimlessness for a quarter of an hour, then swung back to the horse trail and turned down the canyon, intending to hug the south wall all the way to the foot of the trail which had brought him to Canyon de Chelly. If his absence from the Castaneda house had not yet been discovered, he thought this circuitous approach would afford him fair chance of success. If search parties were out and he was caught, there was still a possibility he would succeed in warning the detachment before they encountered the Navajo in full force.

He passed again the uppermost of the hogans, the drum now much fainter than it had been on the upward trip, since the width of the canyon now lay between him and the bench on which the hogans stood.

But the drum was still beating. Lindquist was beginning to feel that every Navajo along the unknown length of de Chelly was engrossed in one of the curious little ceremonials. He was even beginning to think of the possibility of stealing an Indian horse from a carelessly guarded corral somewhere along the line, when he rounded a shoulder of rock and saw Micaela Castaneda a few yards away.

She was sitting on the sand, knees drawn up under her chin, her back against the first lift of the south wall. Her eyes were on the opposite escarpment. Lindquist was not misled by the fact that the ruin he had earlier encountered climbed heavenward there, lighted by a late-rising moon, and that because of the angle one of the little bench groups of hogans seemed to have become a part of the old city, lending life to the ancient dead. It was a scene to catch the fancy and set strange thoughts to pulsing with the beat of the drums still talking up and down the length of the canyon. But the girl's attention on the opposite wall was a little too studied. A little too pointedly she failed to hear the inadvertent small sounds of Lindquist's approach. She was waiting for him. There could be no question about it. And imperturbably, at that.

He moved reluctantly up to her and stood looking down. She didn't turn her head. She let one hand move only enough to indicate the scene across the canyon.

"Beautiful, isn't it?"

A man couldn't answer a thing like that. Not when there were a lot of others which needed answering worse. Lindquist said nothing.

"Father says here you can turn time back. Just as far as you want to. Maybe that's important to him — to anybody who's old. I don't know. But what it seems to me here is that time stands still — that's what I want to do — make time stand still."

"You followed me," Lindquist growled. "That's why the dogs didn't bark. They knew you were with me — behind me — even if I didn't."

The girl ignored him as deliberately as he had ignored her talk of stopping time.

"I don't want anything to happen in Canyon de Chelly from this moment on," she continued softly. "I want it to stay as it is now. The air like this — soft. The quiet. The corn growing, even at night. Not even the dogs barking. Just the Wisdom Drums, forever —"

Lindquist shoved a boot toe into the sand and lifted it. A silver stream ran from the crown of the leather back into the silver sand in the moonlight. He felt mild satisfaction. This was the kind of thing Steve Grayson dreamed up beside a bivouac fire after a day's long ride. And here was Rick Lindquist turning it up in fact, without any effort to speak of at all — and with no wise fellow troopers to haul him out of it with profane malice.

"If this minute's going to last that long," he said, "mind if I sit down?"

The girl turned her head to look at him for the first time. She said nothing until he had sprawled down beside her.

"I didn't follow you," she murmured. "Not all the way. There's only one foot trail above our house by which even a goat could get out of Canyon de Chelly. And you'd never find that. When I got tired I sat down here. I knew you'd have to come back this way."

"You knew I'd escape — or try. You wanted me to. You made it easy for me."

"I — I wasn't sure. I hoped you'd try to get out. But you — you fell without a sound back at the house. It's easy for even a good bowman to make a mistake with a bird-stick. If the string is a little too tight, the blunt arrow cracks the skull. I couldn't tell —"

60

"Mine's just dented," Lindquist said. "But why shoot me down and then deliberately let me escape? Even silencing the dogs so I could move up the canyon."

The girl gestured, including the whole scene before them.

"Doesn't this tell you? Don't you see?" She bent earnestly forward. "What you've come here to do is wrong. Just as wrong as what some of Chief Juanito's men did at Santa Fe and Taos. The Navajo have lived here so long I can't make *them* look at this and understand they must give up *something* to protect this place. It's their home. They're in trouble and they have come back to it for safety. They'll fight more desperately here than anywhere else."

She paused. Her voice dropped, vibrant, low, compelling.

"You — you've never been in Canyon de Chelly before. You can see and hear and understand things the Indians have forgotten — that their grandfathers forgot before them."

Lindquist rubbed the knot on his head over his left ear and studied this girl. She was too much in earnest for him to doubt her sincerity, but she wasn't making too much sense.

"You said something about Wisdom

Drums," he suggested. "If you could get them to talk to me, maybe I could get you figured out."

The girl's eyes widened. "But they *are* talking to you — all of them — from one end of the canyon to the other. They have been ever since you crawled out the window at the house and I knew you were starting up here. They're asking something up there" — she indicated the strip of night sky bounded by the rims of the canyon — "to make you understand so you can make the soldiers understand in turn."

Lindquist blinked. "The Indians at the hogans — the dancers — the rest of them — they all knew I'd slipped out of your house, that I was working past them? You kept them away from me?"

The girl nodded. "If I hadn't pleaded with them for this chance and asked for the drums tonight, you would have had an arrow here" — she thrust her finger against the base of Lindquist's throat — "an arrow with a point on it. And before you were out of our yard!"

Lindquist felt a set of not greatly over-used cells in the back of his brain wither and die. Cells which had been devoted to occasional shadowy creations of a tall, willowy, dignified girl with an appreciation of a military man's problems. He leaned a little closer to Micaela Castaneda and discovered her voice had tightened a little.

"You — you did all of this for me?"

The girl looked at him with recognizable exasperation.

"I was afraid you'd misunderstand! I took precautions, Rick Lindquist!"

She made a little gesture. There was a stir in a cleft in the rock a few yards away. A shadow moved and resolved itself into a rifle-bearing Indian. He crossed quickly to them, the muzzle of his weapon slanted full at Lindquist in a not quite casual sort of way, as if it just might go off any moment, maybe even accidentally. Lindquist didn't like guns in the hands of Indians. He didn't like this. He swore. Micaela grinned maliciously at him, then sobered.

"Sit down, Chin-yi," she said to the Indian. "It's time to talk."

FIVE

The Navajo whom the Castaneda girl called Chin-yi was young. Too young for a seat on the tribal Council. But bitter earnestness, deeply ingrained, made him seem much older. He spoke with a swift fluency and a remarkable ability to translate the poetic phraseology of his native tongue into immensely expressive English. Lindquist resented his appearance, coming as it did when the drum-pulsing silence of Canyon de Chelly and the night seemed to belong to Micaela and himself. But he was forced to listen to the Indian with growing respect and attention.

A crusader talked in this fashion. A preacher of the right kind, maybe. And some of the old mountain men Lindquist had known. Strange hermits who roamed the whole vastness of the West, talking of farms and cities, roads and railroads, as though they themselves would build them or see them built. It became obvious as the Indian spoke that there was a sharp division among the Navajo people. Apparently the older element of the tribe was content

64

to be absorbed in daily living, their minds turned back toward the past. But the younger portion of the tribe was not. *Yanqui* was a word often used since the change at Santa Fe from the old Spanish regime. Not necessarily with hatred, but certainly with distrust.

This was not altogether confined to the Navajo. Lindquist had encountered similar feeling among other tribes. And there was considerable justification for it. The steady penetration of the Western plains and the mountains beyond them by men from across the Missouri was chiefly an adventure. Those in the pack outfits, the hunting parties, and the emigrant wagons were adventurers. Men looking for an unknown something better and richer than the known things they left behind them. Principles of justice and ethics varied with the individual. And there were many who considered the Indian an enemy, without rights and due no consideration.

Lindquist was not inclined to set himself up in judgment on this principle. Even it had some justification. But he understood the distrust of the Navajo. Word must be filtering in constantly from the north of the sporadic war being fought against encroaching wagons and protective soldiery by the horse tribes of the Great Plains. Farther west and south there must be reports of the desert campaigns against the Apache. There could be little doubt in any quarter that the Indian was fighting, and fighting desperately, for his life, his game, and his land.

The Navajo was not yet directly threatened, chiefly because this country was high desert, inhospitable to the whites, and unwanted by them. But something more important was in the balance here. Chin-yi made this plain. The Navajo, like the other nations, were prepared to fight — for their pride and for their immemorial freedom. A group of the younger men was committed to the traditional pattern of tribal warfare — an aggressive carrying of the fight to the enemy. It was this group which had staged the beautifully planned but poorly executed revolt along the upper Rio Grande. It was this group which had urged the retreat of the nation to this canyon, where the spiritual protection of their ancestors was nearly as formidable a defense as the topography of the canyon itself. Nor was this group altogether a troublemaking element. Many were but alarmed and practical men who saw only one way to defend their people.

Chin-yi made it plain he was not a member of this group. He headed a much smaller segment of his people who had little belief in their eventual ability to do so, but who were willing to attempt an agreement with the *yanquis* which would leave themselves and their mesas untouched by the tremendous, brawling migration from the East.

Where the young Navajo failed in finding a word, Micaela supplied it. If both of them failed, they fell back on Lindquist's excellent command of Spanish to make certain he understood them completely. It was an uncomfortable experience. Neither seemed to take into consideration that he was but one man, wholly without authority as regarded the Army, and certainly with no effective means to argue their case among his own people should he be inclined to do so.

And there was the question of initial sympathy. They overlooked this completely also. Lindquist had fought his share of Indians. He had protected himself from their thievery. He had done his level best to outtrade them wherever he could. He had habitually discounted the flowery oratory and overdone posturings of their speech-making before treaty councils and had himself posed out his part and spoken extravagantly without believing for a moment that more than a little said on either side was honest.

This was different. There could be no questioning the utter sincerity of Chin-yi's arguments and his pleas. Lindquist knew Micaela Castaneda, watching so earnestly, would have cut his throat had he doubted the Navajo in the least. In the end he was forced to succumb to the spell of the dark canyon and Chin-yi's appeal as he had already succumbed to the girl's bright and eager beauty.

"All right," he said. "But orders have been issued. The Army's supposed to run you all south into Bosque Redondo. The Army doesn't do much listening to civilians. What can I do?"

"Convince the soldiers — their officers — that they can't do this!" Chin-yi said fiercely. "*This* is our land, not Bosque Redondo. From Canyon de Chelly to the Puerco is our land. From Canyon de Chelly to Black Mountain. Away from it we would die. It's a long way to Bosque Redondo. My people fear the march — as prisoners. The Long Walk they call it already. They will not go!"

"You can turn the soldiers back,"

Micaela added hopefully.

"It's hard enough to convince one man he's making a mistake," Lindquist protested stubbornly. "With an army it's impossible."

"Tonight we would have tried to convince all of the men with you," the girl said. "That's why I asked them all to come to our *estancia*. I would have let them walk here in the canyon as you have done. Chin-yi and I would have talked to them. But only you came."

"You wouldn't have attacked the command?"

The girl smiled a little. "Only as much as we attacked you — to disarm them. Chin-yi had his men on the trail to do this. If they had listened to us afterward, they would not have been harmed."

"If they hadn't?"

The girl shrugged uncomfortably. Chin-yi answered quietly for her.

"We would have killed them. There are many dead in this canyon, señor. Buried and forgotten men. We would have buried your soldiers. They would have disappeared. Who would know where?"

"What good would that have done you? I keep trying to tell you — anything you do to an Army force you'll pay for. I can't seem to make you understand this Army is bigger than all of the Navajo who ever lived!"

Chin-yi shrugged with a trace of a smile.

"It is not a question of how big is the Army. There is no punishment for the death of a man who has merely disappeared, for it is not known as a fact that he is dead. I believe this is the *yanqui* law."

"When it comes to murder, yes. When it comes to an individual. But a whole military command —"

"Is there any difference? I said your soldiers would have disappeared. Believe me, they would never have been found."

Lindquist's temper was shortening.

"The Army has plenty of soldiers!" he snapped.

"The Navajo have plenty of arrows," was the imperturbable reply.

Lindquist rose to his feet. The others rose also. He towered above both of them and felt momentarily good for this before an uncomfortable thought struck him. He wondered if this confidence in superior stature didn't underlie much of the difference his own race found with those it assumed to be inferior. He had lived long enough in Indian country, watching the relationship between the two peoples, to admit this was as believable a reason for the unequal basis of most dealings as any other. He felt guilty for the admission.

Chin-yi turned away without farewell. The sand whispered under his moccasins and the sound faded. The canyon shadows seemed to close in. Lindquist looked at the Spanish girl facing him. He knew what Grayson would do now. What any Army man would do. Here again was something he could not pass upon in judgment. A man was a man and a woman was a woman. Obligations were created between one and the other, and obligations required fulfillment. This girl had asked much of him. She expected much more.

Still, there had to be some fundamental difference in men which made one choose a uniform and a career of certain rewards while another chose sweat-sticking buckskins and the inevitable extinction of the mountain man, the trapper, the hunter, and the scout. Maybe this was that difference. Or a part of it, at least. Or he was a fool. He spoke to Micaela without reaching for her.

"You think I'm going to try this crazy thing you want me to?"

"I can hope for it," she answered quietly. "I can pray for it. I can do everything in

71

my power to see that you turn the soldiers away from Canyon de Chelly."

She looked at him for a moment, then leaned slowly toward him. She had to reach high in the darkness to find his head. He bent to her lips. Even the drums stopped. Lindquist, who had occasionally kissed a woman, was for a long moment kissed by a woman in return.

He was briefly aware of a faint, breathlessly pleasant scent which made him cringe inwardly at the potency of his worn buckskins and long-unwashed body. He felt a smooth cheek lightly against the dusty, stubbled leather of his own. He glimpsed a warmth and softness which were immensely compelling to a man who had chiefly known only hardships and hardness. For a moment he saw with stark clarity the complete emptiness of the thing he had tried to do — of the life he had tried to live.

The challenge and the wonder of crossing into valleys no man of his kind had before seen. The patient tracing of lonesome rivers to the high springs of their beginnings. The growing knowledge, built of day-to-day movement without map or compass, of what lay in the vast land beyond the main channels of the Missouri.

The triumph of body and hard skills against a wilderness and against the Indian. The conviction that largeness of soul could be achieved only in the huge emptiness of the mountain country. These became as nothing.

He felt his own inadequacy in this moment. But he also felt anger. And anger was something with which he was familiar. He seized eagerly upon it, pushing the girl away with more strength of body and principle than he knew he possessed.

"That wasn't necessary," he said, recognizing the source of the strain in him but refusing to admit Rick Lindquist was this much in need of a woman.

The girl stepped back and looked steadily at him. He thought she, also, might be angry. There was that kind of look in her eyes. It could have been hurt. More likely it was stung pride.

"You can believe what you want of me," she said evenly. "But there's one thing I want you to *know* about me —"

Her whole body stiffened. She seemed to grow taller. Her voice lost its softness of a moment before. Steel rang in it.

"There's nothing I won't do to keep soldiers from this canyon. If they come here, there's nothing I won't do to see them killed to the last man. Nothing!"

She turned and strode quickly across the sand, leaving Lindquist looking at the place where she had been, too shaken to break the spell of his own volition, and suddenly considering the things a man might do for a woman. Slowly the sound of the drums rose in the distance and the moment was gone. Lindquist breathed deeply, grateful that Grayson or some of his fellow troopers had not witnessed this. It was bad enough to be among uniforms who considered him a queer one, a hermit, half a savage for his dress and profession. It would be unbearable to be known also as a fool — a fool who did not understand a woman.

Moving thirty yards down the canyon, Lindquist found his horse, led up and left waiting for him. As he pulled into his saddle he tried to estimate how much of the night remained. Two hours, perhaps. And with the rising of the sun the detachment would at least be scouting the rim above him. Some alert trooper — perhaps the impatient Grayson — would spot the message he had written on the sandy floor of the canyon with his apparently aimless wandering before he turned back down to his meeting with Chin-yi and the Castaneda girl.

Two hours to sunrise and an hour for the discovery of the message. It would take him that long to climb the trail to the mesa rim and clear himself of any Navajo sentries along the way. It was just about right. Once he had regained the detachment, the problems of Canyon de Chelly would belong to the Castanedas and the Navajo. Those on the rim would belong to Captain Pfieffer. He would be clear of involvement in either, except as his opinions might be required by the military. And he greatly doubted this under the circumstances.

If a twinge of conscience over an unaccepted obligation to the Spanish girl troubled him later, it could be shrugged off as a man learned to shrug off many such twinges. She had not made sufficient offer to a man who had spent his life in trading with and for the Indians.

SIX

The canyon was no less magnificent from the rim in full daylight than it had been from the sandy floor at night. Lindquist could not keep his eyes from the sheer impossibility of its walls and so rode as close to the lip of the rim as he could contrive. Thus it was that he approached within a quarter of a mile of them before he saw the troopers of the detachment, dismounted and deployed across a promontory ahead. The blue of their uniforms was bright against the red of the country rock.

Crossing a fissure, he angled up toward them and presently had a steep downward view at his left to the canyon floor. A number of brightly dressed Indians — almost certainly women, although the color of the clothing was all a man could go by at this distance — were busily obliterating the diminutive footprints which spelled out the largely drawn word NAVAJO and an arrow pointing down the canyon. The tracks were his, the message the one he had tramped into an open patch of sand the night before.

He paused to watch the work of obliteration below, knowing the soldiers spread out above him on the rocks were watching also. He was agreeably satisfied his message had been seen and read by the detachment. So much of the previous afternoon and night had gone against him — so much of event and circumstance had been beyond his control — that it restored his confidence to know the combined planning of the Castanedas and the Navajo had not been able to circumvent an efficient contact with his command.

Well aware this was actually small cause for vanity, Lindquist was nevertheless grinning over it for lack of any better cause for amusement when the guns above him opened fire without warning. It was the ragged fusillade of veteran soldiery obeying a command to fire at will, each man taking his time to correct sights for perhaps four hundred yards of difficult downward range, squeezing the trigger only with some assurance of target.

Puffs of dust blossomed on the canyon floor. The brightly clad figures there turned faces skyward in an instant of alarm, then began to run with agonizing slowness toward the base of the wall. Here overhang would afford shelter. One figure fell and did not rise again. As others doubled back to render aid, Lindquist kicked his horse into a full, reckless lope up the slippery, slanting stone toward the deployed troopers. And between the animal's clattering, scrambling strides on the treacherous footing he rose high in his stirrups to fling his voice in anger up the slope ahead of him.

"Hold your fire, you idiots! Hold your fire!"

Grayson and Captain Pfieffer lifted themselves up at his hail, but neither passed his order on to the command. The rifle fire continued. Down in the canyon another figure sprawled lifeless on the sand. Lindquist held angrily straight at Grayson and the captain for a moment longer. Then suddenly the whole rim seemed to explode in a hundred small puffs of smoke.

Lead sang angrily in the air and against red stone. It flung a stinging spray over the sprawled troopers. Pfieffer, after a moment of apparent shock, commenced bawling stentorian orders. The troopers began scrambling back toward their horses. From half a hundred hiding places Navajo riflemen broke cover, a whole file of them cutting between Lindquist and the detachment. Small, dark men, scuttling across the rock, vanishing and reappearing, moving with instinctive skill from crevice to crevice.

By the time Pfieffer's force was on its feet and withdrawing, two troopers were down, motionless, and counting the heaviness of the Navajo fire, there were likely others past retreating. However, the majority of the uniforms managed to reach their horses, re-mount, and pound off toward the shelter of timber farther back on the mesa. Lindquist gave over concern for them for concern for himself. He swung into a shallow, slanting depression, thinking he could use it to carry him through the thin Navajo line and so re-join the detachment in the timber. However, he was a fair target. His horse ran into a bullet and died beneath him between one stride and the next.

The animal's head went down without warning. Lindquist came up high out of his saddle. He turned partly in mid-air. Rough sandstone leaped at him. He struck heavily. His forward momentum carried him skiddingly across smooth stone, and he crashed with bone-shaking violence against a huge piece of scab rock broken loose from the mother formation and up-tilted in his path.

The bright morning sun faded and he felt very cold.

Lindquist lay quietly, considering. He didn't think his fall had fully knocked him out. Just stunned him some. He was a hardheaded man and he'd taken falls before. Enough of them to know there wasn't much you could do when you spilled like this but lie where you were in a sort of daze. At least till you'd gotten your breath back. So he took it easy, not fighting, and enjoyed the dreaming, knowing it likely he'd have to suffer some, directly, when stunned senses began to function again.

It was kind of funny, the way it worked. He found he could steer his mind as though it had a wheelbarrow's handles and he could take hold of them and roll it practically anywhere he wished. He thought first of his anger at the stupidity of the soldiers in firing on the party of Indian women on the floor of the canyon. Maybe they had not realized they were women at that distance, but they should have made sure. Or maybe Pfieffer belonged to that sizable school of Indian warfare which considered any Indian fair game in an engagement. This was something he hadn't before considered, and since he had not seen Pfieffer in action, there had been no previous way to know. He was going to pull the captain sharply up on this when he got the chance.

It wasn't that Eric Lindquist wasn't as callous as the next. He pretty near had to be. There were aspects of an Indian woman's life among her own people which were as brutal as her death at the hands of careless white soldiery. There were many things commonplace along the frontier which fell short of accepted gallantry — even of decency — east of the Missouri. Necessarily so. Lindquist figured he was maybe being unreasonably and unprofessionally disturbed by the death of a couple of Indians who had been mistaken for warriors and he realized it, so he knew his anger was not really over this.

So maybe it could be the fact he could have told Captain Pfieffer and Steve Grayson — if he could have gotten to them — that the Navajo were very probably in contact with them, waiting for a wrong move or even a chance to attack, even if they couldn't be seen. Maybe the military folly of inviting attack by an enemy of unknown strength and on unfamiliar ground was what really galled him. But this didn't seem to hold water, either. He wasn't enough of a military man to pass judgment on a pair of apparently competent enough officers, and there was the incontrovertible old rule of skirmish that striking the first blow was generally a move to advantage.

With stubborn reluctance Lindquist finally came around to thinking about Micaela Castaneda, and he knew that here was where his anger rooted. The heat in him increased because this was something he didn't want to do, but he found himself thinking of her as he had thought of a tall girl with a level head on her shoulders when he was younger. He was thinking of her as he had not permitted himself to think of her down on the canyon floor with the night sky overhead and the drums in the distance and the warmth of her body close to him.

Captain Pfieffer's rifle attack on the women below angered him, in fact, because it was the first skirmish in a battle now certain to echo the length of Canyon de Chelly, and the Spanish girl who had been born here wanted no battle in her canyon. Somehow, contrary to the stubbornness of his common sense, Lindquist had wanted to prevent conflict for her, even when he was certain this was impossible. He was a fool. A crazy fool. This was the kind of reasonless reaction a youngster like Steve Grayson might be expected to show. But not a sobered man like Eric Lindquist.

Rick stirred a little to see if he yet could. The stir hurt some. He swore with feeling and opened his eyes, figuring that, hurt or no, he'd gotten his breath back a little and it was time he climbed back onto his feet. With his eyes open he blinked and immediately regretted the personal acridity of his oath. Micaela Castaneda was bent above him. She had on a long, full skirt and an intricately embroidered blouse which seemed ridiculously out of place until he realized he was not lying against a big rock on the openness of the mesa, but again in a bedroom of the Castaneda *estancia*.

He had been a long time getting back his wind. A heavy growth of beard stubbled his cheeks and chin. His belly was flat and empty. He took a long, deep breath. Slowly and uncertainly he raised himself to a sitting position. A Navajo woman he had not seen approached and surveyed him critically. He didn't think she was at all friendly. She turned to Micaela and asked a question in her own tongue. Micaela shrugged with a small, uncertain frown.

"I don't know," she answered softly in Spanish. "So long delirious — Father says he may never recover —"

"*Sí,*" the Navajo woman agreed with evident relish. She made an unmistakable gesture toward her own head. "*Loco . . .*"

"*Loco* my eye!" Lindquist said with some resentment. "I'm as sane as either of you!"

The Navajo woman's traditionally immobile face mirrored an astonishment so complete as to reveal painfully to Lindquist the extent of the delirium to which Micaela had referred. The Indian woman ran from the room, her excited chattering ringing through the rest of the house. Micaela had leaned over and pushed with small hands against Lindquist's chest, urging him to lie back down.

"Please be quiet! You've been very sick. Your head . . ."

He put an unsteady hand to the crown of his skull and found a great bald patch sheared into the thick mane of his hair. In the center of this was the healing crust of an irregular, staggering big scalp wound.

"Brained myself against that rock," he muttered.

"Don't try to talk!" Micaela cut in quickly. "You've been too sick."

"How long?" Lindquist asked, and stubbornly repeated the question when she didn't answer. "How long?"

"Eight days. Nine, today. Now you *must* be quiet!"

Nine days! Lindquist figured he'd been a devil of a lot of trouble to somebody. He thought the drawn look on the girl's face explained well enough who. But he had to be sure.

"The detachment?"

"The soldiers retreated," she answered. She wearily brushed a strand of hair back from her face. "Back across the mesa. And they sent to Santa Fe for help. Another company has joined them now. The trader from Taos — the famous one — he's with them too."

"Carson? Kit Carson's here?"

She nodded. Lindquist rubbed the sole of one unbooted foot up the shank of the other leg under the blanket covering him. In so doing he discovered he had been stripped to the knit undersuit he had learned to wear beneath his buckskins in the high country. So clad, he was not at his best. He resented this invasion of his privacy very much. The more so because he didn't know who had perpetrated it. And he couldn't ask.

"My clothes. Where are my clothes?"

"Tomorrow. We'll find them tomorrow."

She seemed quite firm about it. But with Kit Carson on the mesas above the canyon, too many tomorrows had passed already. Lindquist flung the blanket back and swung his feet to the floor. The movement sent a dull ache through his head, but his voice was steady enough.

"We'll find them now!" he said.

SEVEN

The girl stared at him without humor, then turned and left the room. Lindquist rose and crossed unsteadily to a stand above which hung an excellent mirror. A caricature looked out of the glass at him. When he recovered from the first shock he decided wryly that the majority of the apparent damage had been done by the shears which had cut the hair away from the wound on his head. He thought he looked like the victim of a very clumsy and unprofessional job of scalping. If Micaela had done this, certainly some malice must have been involved. It would be a long season before he would look presentable, even in a campaign camp, without a hat.

Presently the Navajo woman re-entered with his clothes and dumped them on the bed. His boots had been carefully oiled to limp pliantness. His buckskins had been mended and cleaned, apparently by the patient process of pounding fine clay into them and then brushing it off, taking the dirt with it. Their rankness was gone. They had a fresh earth smell about them, like dust after rain.

Before he finished dressing the Navajo woman entered again with food. He ate and felt better. And he wanted to talk to Micaela. Crossing to the door, he moved out into the hall. The main rooms of the house were empty. He stepped out onto the narrow veranda and halted, struck by the scene he encountered here without warning. It was something few white men if any had ever seen, to their great fortune.

Covering the whole of the little bench on which the Castaneda house stood was a solid, silent mass of Indians. Not the women and children and old ones — the usual company a tribe turned out to create an effect. These were the men — the fighting men — of the Navajo. An army, grimly facing the house, facing him. Lindquist's throat felt dry. He swallowed with some effort.

Estimation of so close-packed a mass could not be accurate. Two thousand — maybe half again as many. It was almost unbelievable. Chin-yi had not been idly boasting when he had said the Navajo were strong. Neither had Micaela. Lindquist wondered if any other tribe in the country could make a turnout like this. He could think of none who could do half so well. He thought of the thirty men with which

Captain Pfieffer, Grayson, and himself had set out from Santa Fe. Thirty men to capture, subdue, and lead this horde to punishment. It was almost funny.

This was what made trouble in New Mexico Territory. It was new and unknown. The Army and the government acted too often without information. This, for instance, was the Navajo nation, usually carelessly dismissed as scattered desert sheepherders. Maybe they were sheepherders, but what was important was that there were more than two thousand of them. Even sheepherders in this number could be dangerous and powerful. Even if Kit Carson, in reinforcing Pfieffer, had secured every soldier under arms in the territory, the odds here would still be better than ten to one.

Lindquist slowly crossed the veranda and stepped into the yard. Pablo Castaneda, together with Chin-yi and three other Navajo who were apparently household help, made a small group before the house. Lindquist joined them. Micaela, who had been standing a little apart, moved in near her father.

"What is this?" Lindquist asked her quietly.

She shook her head. "We don't know.

They started pouring in here in the last ten minutes. We had no warning. They want something, of course. What, we don't know. They seem to be waiting for a talker — a spokesman."

Lindquist frowned. Presently a stir began among the Indians. Some of them pointed up the canyon. A single horseman, lance held high, was riding toward the house at breakneck speed. Chin-yi and the Castanedas exchanged uneasy glances. The rear ranks of the Indian crowd opened to form a lane. The rider pounded through this without slackening speed. The front ranks parted. Man and horse burst through to pull up in a rearing halt before the group at the edge of the veranda.

"Chief Juanito!" Micaela murmured.

Her father nodded. "Looks like he's to be the talker. This is important, then, Micaela!"

As the rearing horse came down, the Indian drove his lance head deep into the sod of the dooryard with a fierce downward stroke. The shaft of the weapon vibrated gently as he reined away from it. Chief Juanito dismounted. Except for his fierceness, he wasn't a prepossessing figure. A relatively small, dark man who would have suffered greatly in physical comparison to

Washakie, Mangas, and Ouray — great men of other tribes with whom Lindquist was familiar. But perhaps he was the greatest of them all. At least in this moment. He had two thousand men at his back.

He glowered at the little party facing him. He spoke sharply, and after a moment's hesitation the three household Navajo crossed to merge with their fellow tribesmen. Juanito spoke again, this time to Chin-yi, but received a negative shake of the head. The young Navajo remained standing with the Castanedas. Although he could not understand the language, Lindquist grasped what was happening.

Micaela had said Chin-yi was the leader of a small group of the younger men. Juanito was chief of the tribe. There were enemy soldiers on the mesa and he was calling on Chin-yi to surrender control of his group for the good of the whole. Something of this nature. And Chin-yi, perhaps out of concern for the Castanedas, was refusing the chief's demand. This was sufficiently plain for Lindquist to be partially prepared for what followed.

The chief suddenly snatched his lance from the ground and cast it swiftly. The keen, slender head struck Chin-yi in the chest, transfixing him. As he grasped the shaft of the weapon with both hands in a futile effort to ease the hurt, Micaela cried out and leaped toward him. Lindquist caught her and jerked her roughly back, twisting her arm savagely to keep her from struggling or crying out.

Pablo Castaneda stared impassively at Chin-yi as the young Indian took one faltering step and fell. Juanito spoke, using explosive Spanish.

"There is only one chief of the Navajo! There is only one enemy!"

He turned to the mass of men behind him. There was a strong murmur of approval, although it was plain Chin-yi had many friends in the crowd. A soft chant, without recognizable form, began among the most enthusiastic of the chief's followers, slowly increasing in tempo and volume as one after another of the Navajo took it up. Juanito swung back to Lindquist and the Castanedas. He indicated Chin-yi's body with the toe of one moccasin.

"He wanted to trade for peace. Juanito will trade for peace too — with blood!"

"You make a mistake, Juanito," Pablo Castaneda said quietly. "The Council is mistaken to let you make it. I, your friend, tell you this."

Juanito made a quick gesture of a cut throat with one finger.

"Friend!" he spat. He pointed at Lindquist. "This *yanqui* is a friend also, I suppose?"

Lindquist pushed Micaela behind him and moved easily forward to face the Navajo chief. He let his eyes run over the man for a long moment of deliberately insolent silence before he spoke.

"I could be," he agreed. "I have been asked to be. But why should I? I want only wise men for friends."

Juanito's color darkened. The chant among the Indians quieted so all could hear this exchange. The chief studied Lindquist carefully.

"Let the great *yanqui* tell the stupid Navajo what *is* wise, then," he said acidly.

Lindquist pointed to the rim of the canyon wall looming above them. All eyes tilted skyward with the gesture.

"Soldiers are there," he said. "Many soldiers. If there are not enough, more soldiers will come. More soldiers than the grains of the sand on the floor of your canyon. And Carson is with them. The trader from Taos all Indians say is the wisest chief among the *yanquis*."

Juanito nodded, waiting him out.

"Carson will bring the soldiers into de Chelly. Your scouts have told you this. You've got to do something. That's why you're here."

Juanito nodded again. Bending suddenly, without warning, he tore the lance from Chin-yi's body and brandished it fiercely. Behind him Lindquist heard Micaela draw a sharp breath of alarm. Her father murmured a quick caution.

"This canyon belongs to the Navajo!" Juanito said hoarsely. "No soldiers. No whites. Only Navajo!"

"The soldiers don't want a war with your people," Lindquist told him evenly. "*Yanqui* soldiers don't like to die. I know. I know what's in their hearts. I came here with the first of them. What they want is those of your men who spilled blood along the Rio Grande. They'll get those men, Juanito. Those are their orders. They'll get them if they have to fight their way from one end of your canyon to the other to do it. What kind of a chief will risk all of his people for a few he knows have done a wrong?"

Lindquist's lips felt dry when he got this out. The slender lance in the hand of the Navajo chief was dancing nervously, and he had already seen how swiftly it could strike. He wet his lips and kept his eyes on the muscles of Juanito's upper arm. It was an unnecessary precaution. The chief drove the head of the weapon again into the sod at his feet and folded his arms.

"A chief thinks for all his people," he said slowly, making his first apparent effort to be reasonable and completely understood. "He bleeds for them in their trouble and he ends that trouble when he can find a way. I am Juanito. Always I have believed in fighting when there is an enemy. But if there is another safe path to peace, I would take it. Now, hear me! How can the soldiers find who among my people were on the Rio Grande? How can I find who they were? Will they tell me and lose their lives? Will they surrender to the soldiers? Will their women and children tell who they are? Will their brothers? I could give the soldiers men, but they would not all be the right ones. The innocent would suffer. The guilty would go unpunished. Is this justice?"

He paused and gripped the upright lance before him with both hands, clenching them tightly.

"And this is thinking only of today. I think of other seasons too. Many *yanquis* will call Juanito a bad chief. Maybe this is so. But not because my heart is bad. The soldiers have been ordered to drive us all from Canyon de Chelly — to take us all to Bosque Redondo. That is what they want — not the surrender of those who made the trouble on the Rio Grande."

Juanito's head lifted proudly to the rock walls rising to the sky.

"This is the house of our fathers. They want to drive us from it. They want to break our spirits so that we will never fight again. If not this season, they will come among us again the next. Or the next after that. Isn't this the real truth?"

The Indian's honesty was compelling. Lindquist felt obliged to repay him in kind. He shook his head slowly.

"I don't know. It's a long way to Washington. No man can guess what the white chiefs there are thinking. But it seems to me that if the Navajo don't fight, there'd be no need to break them — now or later."

"That's *your* thinking," Juanito said. "You are here — in Canyon de Chelly. Perhaps even you are a friend to the Navajo. But as you say, it is a long way to the chiefs in Washington. And the Navajo must protect themselves. Take Juanito's words to the soldiers. Tell them that if they go back across the mesas they can send my promise to their chiefs that there will be no more trouble with the Navajo until the Day-after-the-Ending. But tell them, also, that if they enter this canyon they die!"

Lindquist shrugged a little and started to turn away, clinging to a mountain man's conviction that, however a parley with Indians went, it could be considered a success if white participants walked away from it with their lives. Juanito stopped him and indicated the Castanedas.

"The old one and the woman will go with you," he said.

Lindquist glanced at Micaela's father. Castaneda had known this was coming. But the old man could not keep a stricken look from his eyes. Loyalty, Lindquist realized, not interest in land or in any principle of right and wrong, had made Castaneda stick by the Navajo. When they deserted him, he was alone. This was towering ingratitude. His roots were sunk as deeply into the red sands of de Chelly as were those of the Navajo.

Lindquist swept his hand widely to include the whole bench occupied by the *estancia*.

"This is the old one's land," he pointed out. "This is the woman's home."

Juanito shrugged uncomfortably.

"Navajo land too. Navajo home. The old one and the woman are not Navajo. We talk of war, not of justice. Let them suffer first."

Castaneda touched Lindquist's arm. "It is of no use, señor," he said heavily. "They have the horses saddled and ready for us at the corral. We'd better go. In an hour the floor of the canyon won't be safe for any of us."

Micaela's eyes leaped from her father to Lindquist and then to Juanito. Her lips compressed. She ran across to face the chief, pausing for a moment as though in an attempt to find words for the fury within her. Finding none, she swung suddenly with all the strength of her body, and her hand exploded across the Navajo's cheek, leaving a slowly darkening stain of violence where her palm struck. Juanito seized her savagely, but before Lindquist could leap forward to interfere, the Indian slowly released the girl.

"The little one feels better than any of us now," Juanito said quietly. "She has said what is really in her heart."

Tears sprang up in the girl's eyes. Lindquist took her arm. Her father moved up to her other side. The three of them started toward the horses waiting at the corral. Behind them the chant began again among the massed Navajo.

EIGHT

A quarter of the way up the south wall of the canyon, a twist of the trail looped out to a point overlooking the buildings of the Castaneda *estancia*. As Lindquist approached this with Micaela and her father, he could hear the chanting of the Navajo pulsing with quickened cadence and strength. And he could smell smoke.

When they came to the overlooking bend of the trail, they halted. The house below was an immense pyre. Outbuildings, corrals, and fencing had already been knocked down and added to it. When the flames died, there would be nothing on the bench but ash and the tracks of the hundreds of Indians dancing with ever-swifter rhythm about the flames. The patience, the long dreaming and the building, the happiness the Castanedas had known here — all were gone.

Lindquist's head ached abominably. He gingerly put his fingers to the drying scar on his scalp and wrinkled his nose against the acridity of the rising smoke. Micaela, beside him, stared dry-eyed down into the canyon.

"Why?" she murmured. "Why?"

Lindquist knew no real reason except that these were Indians — savages. This seemed insufficient, an explanation for nothing. But he could find no other. Pablo Castaneda was wiser — perhaps because his hurt was greater.

"They are frightened," he said sadly. "They are going to be hunted like animals, and they know it. They are going to have to live in holes in the rocks — hiding — without food and water. Many will die. They need something good to remember when that time comes. That's why they do this. It is something good to remember — the fire they lighted to burn everything that isn't Navajo out of Canyon de Chelly forever."

"But it's our canyon too!" Micaela protested bitterly. "They've been our friends. They've never hated us before."

"They don't hate us now," the old man said wearily.

"You aren't Navajo; that's it," Lindquist suggested.

"It is as simple as that." Pablo Castaneda nodded. "One doesn't think about it often. The hair is darker, coarser. The color of the skin. The tongue they speak. It comes as a surprise to realize that among the Indians it is a great thing to be an Indian. It comes as a surprise to see their pride. The padres taught much of goodness where they could here — mostly along the Rio Grande. They teach still. But among the Navajo as among the other tribes, there is only one real goodness — to be Navajo — to be Indian."

Castaneda looked up at the balance of the cliff hanging above them and gestured toward it.

"It is still a long climb to the top of the mesa."

Lindquist clucked to his horse and took up the lead again, leaving the girl and the old man to ride behind him with some privacy for the shock of their loss.

An hour later Lindquist looked back into the canyon again from the rim of the mesa. Overhang now sheltered the location of the Castaneda homestead. Smoke rolling above an inaccessible portion of the rim revealed that the fire still burned below. What caught his attention was movement on the visible portion of the canyon floor. A mass of Navajo was streaming up it like a river in reverse. And as the Indians moved, small parties in twos and threes and dozens split off from it. Each of these vanished into crevices and side fissures in the canyon walls. The whole effect was of the Indian force shrinking and vanishing before his eyes, swallowed and absorbed by the red mother rock of de Chelly.

Here was a foretaste of what the military would encounter. An enemy which knew its ground. A fluid enemy, appearing and vanishing at will. An enemy apparent only in small groups against which there could be neither victory nor defense. A promise of a kind of fighting which could cost many lives and accomplish nothing. Lindquist stared down into the canyon, wondering if the genius of even a Carson was equal to this. He started a little when Castaneda spoke at his elbow.

"Señor, look . . ."

Lindquist turned. A meadow of thin sod overlay the mesa rock to their right, extending back from the rim to the nearest fringe of mesa-top timber, slightly blued by distance. At this point of nearest approach, filing out of the trees at a service lope in columns of fours, standard-bearers in the lead, came cavalrymen. Somehow their tight, military precision, visible even at this distance, seemed more pagan than the chanting and the dancing he had seen on the floor of the canyon. Lindquist spoke to his horse. The Castanedas followed him across the meadow toward the advancing party.

Midway across the meadow the cavalry-men pulled up to await their arrival. Pfieffer, Grayson, and another officer were among those who rode out a little in advance. Lindquist recognized the fourth man and scowled. Somehow he had hoped Carson's unusually involved personal affairs would not permit the chief of scouts actually to manage this campaign. It was one thing to have a detachment operating with Carson's counsel and advice available. It was quite another to have Carson himself present in the field. Lindquist tried to figure out why he didn't want his superior here. It was hard going.

Like almost every other man who had ever known the little trader from Taos, Lindquist subscribed to the legend already growing to immense size about the figure of Kit Carson. This subscription was, in fact, the very material out of which much of the legend was built — the respect and admiration held for Carson by those who knew and had worked with him.

It was possible, Lindquist realized, that he was himself so sure of the impregnable position into which the Navajo had retired that he was afraid his friend from Taos was starting out on one Indian campaign he couldn't successfully conclude — a campaign which could do Carson no good professionally and which might work great harm on the man's legend. Or maybe it was that he believed the whole basis of this campaign was wrong and so disliked seeing Carson involved in it for this reason. The man from Taos knew Indians and their country and Indian warfare as did no other. He was shrewd and stubborn and had repeatedly proven himself invincible. He had been ordered to transport the Navajo nation to Bosque Redondo. He would carry out his orders if he had to pry each one individually from the rocks of Canyon de Chelly.

Riding toward the military group, Lindquist decided he knew why he regretted Carson's presence. There was now little possibility of a compromise which would benefit the Navajo. Only Kit Carson would be more stubborn than Juanito of the Navajo. Compromises were impossible between stubborn men.

Carson was the first to speak as Lindquist's group rode up, but not before he had run shrewdly appraising eyes over the Castanedas — with particular attention to Micaela.

"Well, Rick," he said with open amusement, "I told Captain Pfieffer you'd turn up directly — and with the information we needed. But I've got to admit I didn't expect you to show up in such charming company."

Carson laughed. He swept his cap from his fine head of black hair and bowed low in his saddle with an easy gallantry unlooked for in a man in buckskin. The Spanish girl warmed visibly to him, although Lindquist knew both of the Castanedas must feel that the leader of this military force came close to being personally responsible for the destruction of their *estancia* at the hands of the Navajo.

Watching him now, it seemed likely much of Carson's effectiveness lay in the fact there was always the unexpected about him. With some reluctance Lindquist made a formal introduction of the officers, learning in the process that the fourth man in Carson's party was Captain Carey, commanding the reinforcements sent out to bolster Pfieffer's original command. Presentations briefly over, Lindquist reported Chief Juanito's message and the apparent activities of the Navajo in de Chelly. Carson was immediately sympathetic to the loss sustained by the Castanedas.

"Dealing with Indians is often thankless, sir," he told the old man. "They make mistakes in judgment, the same as we do. And their tribal religious beliefs drive them to some actions very hard for whites to understand. If that isn't enough source of trouble, they're the most practical people on the face of the earth. They'll do things — make sacrifices on a long-range basis — that would never occur to us."

"I know," Castaneda agreed. "I believe by now I know Indians better than I understand my own people — or yours."

"My father and I are almost Navajo," Micaela added. "We have lived a long time among them, Colonel. We've been their friends — they have been ours. That's what makes their driving us out so unbelievable!"

"Don't worry about it, Miss Castaneda," Carson told the girl earnestly. "Before we're through with Chief Juanito's people you'll be back on your ranch."

"You seem very sure," Micaela said.

Carson nodded. "I am. I've sent for some Ute scouts. If the Navajo turn stubborn, we'll turn the Utes loose on them — promise them they can keep all the prisoners they take. They'll make the Navajo rebuild your house for you. Now, let's get back to our camp. You look a little in need of rest, ma'am. And Rick Lindquist and I have a long talk coming."

Carson's camp was geometric, a bivouac of military tents in strict alignment, a stock corral, and a supply dump. Spartan and efficient, without litter or disorganization. Steve Grayson, grinning at his agility in cutting out not only Lindquist but Carey and Pfieffer as well, turned his quarters over to the Castanedas and they vanished into the tent. Carson drew Lindquist away from the cavalry officers and with a dozen blunt questions learned most of what else Lindquist knew of the Navajo position. The chief of scouts chewed his mustache thoughtfully.

"Easiest thing would be to start a big force at the head of this canyon of theirs," he said. "Maybe with a couple of mountain guns for support. Funny how effective a cannon is — even a little one — with an enemy which had never heard a cannon fire before."

"It's all right to make a noise, but even a cannon's no good unless it hits the enemy. And the Navajo are going to be hard to hit."

"We can hit them if we have to, Rick,"

Carson said. "Now, we could march this force right down the canyon to its mouth, leaving clean country behind it. That would permanently cure any trouble with these Indians."

"It would cure the Indians too!" Lindquist growled. "There wouldn't be any Navajo left. Is that what you want?"

Carson looked sharply at Lindquist for a moment, then smiled and put a hand upward at an angle to Rick's shoulder.

"Look, Rick," he said quietly, "things are changing out here. It isn't like it was a few years ago. In those days a few of us like you and me who happened to be out here in the high country just did what we figured was best and let it go at that. Now this is all claimed territory. This is the camp of an Army command. I'm even a pro tem colonel as chief of scouts. That makes us official — government agents — acting for the whole country. And back in Washington some gents are tired of the country suffering from the so-called mistakes of scattered buckskin blunderers like you and me!"

"Yeah!" Lindquist snorted. "Now they want to make our mistakes for us — all at once and from their desks in Washington!"

Carson shrugged. "I admit it looks that

way sometimes. You know yourself that I've quit the Army a couple times over one fool thing or another. But good or bad, Rick, the government's at least gotten around to having a policy when it comes to dealing with the Indians. That's more than it ever had before. And it's up to us to make that policy stick. If it doesn't, the tribes aren't going to have any respect for white government and the mountain country's going to be set back twenty years of needless fighting!"

"Then you are going to try driving the Navajo out of Canyon de Chelly — you're going to hunt them all down. Just because a few of the younger ones were mixed up in the Taos rebellion you're going to try making them all pay for it!"

"Those are my orders, Rick."

Lindquist drew a long breath. He knew what he was doing. He knew his risks and the certainty of his eventual wage. With even the high desert beginning to attract settlement and the buds of stable government, a buckskin man's one hope of eating regularly lay in maintaining some kind of connection with the Army. Military operations required competent scouts and would continue to require them for some time. And military pay to a civilian was good. Still, a man had to retain some of the freedoms he had cultivated in the mountains. He had to measure values against one another. And for the moment Eric Lindquist wasn't hungry.

"Better find yourself another scout, Kit," he said sourly.

Carson didn't seem too surprised.

"You quit and I'll have to report it, Rick. The Army won't want you again."

"I got along before there was any Army this far west."

"Sure," Carson agreed. "Maybe you'd get along now. I don't know. But look at the spot you put me in."

"I didn't put you anyplace, Kit. You rode your own horse out here."

"I don't mean that. You know how I operate, just how strong a force I have here, what my orders are. Very valuable information, Rick. If you joined the Navajo with it, I might not be able to budge them at all."

"I didn't say I aimed to join the Navajo," Lindquist protested.

"You might, just the same," Carson persisted pleasantly. "You're just stubborn enough to figure that maybe this is one time the Indians are right. If I gave you a chance to go over to them and you make trouble, folks would be calling Kit Carson

111

the thickheadedest man in New Mexico inside of a week. And they'd be able to prove it. I can't risk that."

"What you going to do then?" Lindquist asked bluntly. "Put me under arrest?"

"You catch on quick, Rick." Carson smiled. "That's it. Technical arrest. Sort of privately — to me. I don't want to mix those kids in officers' uniforms into this till I've had a chance to march some of the ginger out of them. They're too blasted important for their own good right now. They might take this arrest business too seriously. Be kind of uncomfortable for you."

"Maybe you can't make it stick, Kit," Lindquist suggested.

"Maybe not," Carson agreed. "Just have to take my chances, I reckon."

He turned away, leaving Eric Lindquist wondering just exactly what it was he wanted to do.

NINE

Carson spent the better part of the rest of the day crosslegged beside a smooth slab of stone, working out a pair of rough field maps. Pfieffer and Carey and Steve Grayson sat most of the time with him. Twice they called Pablo Castaneda over to clarify a detail. They ignored Lindquist, each of the young officers taking his cue from Carson in this. There was no attempt to shield what they were doing from Lindquist's attention, and he was permitted to roam restlessly about the camp, irritatedly aware of the close personal surveillance Carson kept clamped upon him.

By midafternoon the maps were complete. Probably the first detailed charts of Canyon de Chelly and its tributaries ever drawn. Using them as a basis, Carson began issuing his orders. Pfieffer and Grayson pulled out with half of the command in a long circling movement designed to bring them to the head of Canyon del Muerto, chief tributary of de Chelly, which Pablo Castaneda said branched off about five miles above the mouth of the main chasm. This party was to enter del Muerto at its head and descend its length, driving any Indians it encountered ahead of it. Reaching a juncture with the main canyon, the party was to proceed on to its mouth and seal off Navajo escape by this route.

Half an hour after the departure of the first party Captain Carey started west with the balance of the company, leaving only a token force in camp with Carson to protect the supplies there. Carey was to proceed to the mouth of the canyon and travel up the main course to its head, driving any Indians encountered ahead of him and so up onto the open mesa crown, where they would necessarily have to surrender.

It was sound generalship, typical of Carson. Its single flaw was that Lindquist, admittedly suspected by Carson, had been permitted to absorb the principle of the proposed campaign and much of its detail. If he had possessed information valuable to the Navajo before, he was rich with it now.

Micaela Castaneda came from the quarters afforded her in Grayson's tent to watch Carey's detachment leave. Lindquist found himself standing beside her. She looked somberly up at him.

"So the Long Walk has begun!" she breathed.

"For the Navajo — to Bosque Redondo?" he asked, then answered himself: "Maybe . . ."

"Maybe!" the girl said sharply. "What chance do they have?"

"I don't know," Lindquist told her defensively. "They know how to fight. They were born knowing how to fight. And this is their country. There must be some chance. I saw at least two thousand Navajo warriors down there in the canyon. There are only about a hundred and fifty cavalrymen."

"There are closer to seven thousand Navajo altogether," the girl corrected. "And the women and children — they'll fight as hard as their men if they have to."

Micaela's eyes brightened for a moment. De Chelly seemed to cast a spell over those who knew it, so that a strange kinship was generated which transcended lines of blood and race, creating a curious brotherhood to which this girl belonged. The moment passed. Micaela shrugged heavily and nodded across the camp.

"That's Kit Carson over there. What chance does any Indian force have against him?"

Lindquist shrugged. The girl looked

across at Carson for a long moment, then returned to Grayson's tent. Lindquist drifted across the camp. He passed the pile of duffel on which Carson was sitting but didn't stop. Carson flipped a twig after him to draw his attention.

"Rick . . ."

Lindquist turned reluctantly back. Carson made another place on the pile of duffel. Lindquist ignored it and remained standing.

"Quit acting like a gored buffalo!" Carson grunted. "You and me have fought Indians before."

"To save our skins or somebody else's skins. To get back stolen horses or a fur shipment or run down a pack of killers. But not just for some Army pay."

"Indians are Indians; a job's a job," Carson insisted.

"I've known a few Indians who were folks, Kit — and so have you!" Lindquist found his voice suddenly heated and a little unsteady. "I've known a few Indians who had a right to live where their ancestors and their gods are. I told you — I don't like your stinking, Washington-ordered job. I'm taking my orders from here!"

Lindquist banged his fist against his

chest to indicate himself with a violence even he found surprising. Carson blinked. He didn't seem particularly displeased. In fact, he seemed curiously satisfied. Lindquist was puzzled. Carson came to his feet and reached out his hand.

"Looks like you're really getting your dander up, Rick. Maybe I'm taking chances where I shouldn't. Reckon you'd better give me your gun."

Lindquist hesitated a moment, then pulled off his belt and handed it across. It seemed unnecessary to tell Carson the Navajo had already relieved him of powder, shot, and caps. If it made the colonel feel better to have possession of the empty and useless weapon, he was welcome to it. It would do no harm for him to believe he had pulled Rick Lindquist's teeth.

Carson pushed the gun into the duffel pile and stood up. His grin had gotten markedly wicked. He glanced across the camp toward Grayson's tent.

"Think I'll have a little talk with that girl you found. Any objections, Rick?"

"No," Lindquist said shortly. "Why should there be?"

Carson grinned at him.

"That's something I don't aim to tell you," he said. "If you haven't got reasons of your own, you're a bigger fool than you've a right to be!"

He laughed at his own humor and walked away. Lindquist glared after him.

Supper fires were small and extinguished early at Carson's order to avoid drawing more than necessary attention to the now understaffed camp. Lindquist found his gear among the duffel Pfieffer's party had brought up. He spread his blankets and rolled into them. He slept fitfully. Deep in the small hours he wakened to hear voices from Carson's darkened camp — muted voices, barely audible in the silence over the sleeping camp. They would have meant nothing except they were the voices of men in parley, and the heavy inflections of the tongue of the Southern Utes was unmistakable among them. Lindquist flipped back his blankets and rose noiselessly.

Carson had mentioned employing Ute marauders to the Castanedas in promising them the return of their *estancia*, but none of the strategy worked out with the cavalry officers earlier in the day had included the Utes. Lindquist had until now believed Carson had reconsidered his earlier intention. Turning slave-hunting Utes loose on the already harassed Navajo made further indecision impossible. This could be the way Carson and the fat men in Washington conducted a campaign against an Indian nation guiltless of the crimes of a few. But it wouldn't do for Rick Lindquist. Not by a damned sight!

The hell with Carson's sly inference he was a Navajo-lover, a champion of the Indian. This wasn't so, as some old wounds and considerable recollection betrayed beyond proof. But even out here a man had to live with himself, and Eric Lindquist could not be a party to this campaign and continue to do so. Even the devil had his due, and the majority of the Navajo were a long way from being devils.

He slipped across the camp, part of the way to Grayson's tent, where the Castanedas slept. Before he reached the canvas he changed his mind. If he could be of any aid to the Navajo in the canyon without betraying his blood — if this was what he eventually attempted — the Castaneda girl would hear of it. If he did not do this, she needn't know he had ever considered it. Meanwhile, if he said nothing to her now, she would know nothing and therefore be unable to reveal his intentions inadvertently.

A military sentry was on duty at the

main supply heap of the camp. With some difficulty Lindquist located another near the loosely corralled horses. This second guard was bolstered by a tall Indian looking to the ponies ridden into the camp by the Ute delegation now with Carson.

Doubling back to the supplies, Lindquist approached the sentry there like a night shadow. The man sensed rather than saw or heard him. He pivoted so swiftly that the barrel of his carbine struck Lindquist on the thigh. He opened his mouth in startled challenge, but before he could voice it Lindquist struck him. A clean, loose, finely calculated swing to the point of the man's slack jaw. The sentry's head snapped back and he went down. Lindquist caught the carbine as it fell and swiftly stripped the cavalryman's bandoleer from him. After so much of indecision, the smooth precision of this minor victory filled Lindquist with more than necessary satisfaction.

Rummaging swiftly in the duffel, he found another belt, completely equipped, together with a good pair of officer's pistols. He belted these on and circled the camp toward the horses with a rising elation in him. He found he was grinning, his lips pulled back tightly across his teeth, and sobered with instant self-accusation. A

120

man didn't like this sort of thing. He just did it because he had to.

An inadvertent roll of gravel against stone underfoot drew the second sentry's attention, and the Ute with the ponies stiffened guardedly. Lindquist drew a pistol but left it uncocked and hunched in close against a small piñon. The sentry, probably glad enough for chance at movement away from his confining post, moved obligingly close. He yelped as Lindquist stepped into the open, but a downward sweep of the pistol barrel cut the sound off abruptly. Dropping to one knee, Lindquist cocked his weapon and swung it toward the Ute horse guard.

The Indian was in a dodging run across the camp. Lindquist fired carefully. The Ute stumbled under the drive of the bullet and skidded on his face almost into the entry of Carson's tent as the flap of the shelter burst open and Carson and his Ute guests spilled out.

Lindquist ran lightly to the corral, breached it, and swung onto the back of the first frightened horse to bolt through the breach. He had scant enough control of the animal by mere handholds in its mane, but the rest of the camp stock was following his mount, and pursuit seemed unlikely if not completely impossible for the moment. Carson apparently recognized this. His shout rose over the rattle of the first shots flung after Lindquist:

"Hold your fire!"

Excited troopers, spilled from sleep, were hard to restrain. Carson bellowed again:

"Hold your fire, confound it! The girl's gone too! He must have her with him!"

Lindquist's horse skittered unbelievably down a slant of bare red stone, hit better footing on thin turf again, and carried him on out of earshot. He clung automatically to the animal's back, his mind wholly engrossed with the possible whereabouts and intent of Micaela Castaneda. He had not considered the possibility she might also escape from Carson's camp, and he swore over it.

In the first place, he doubted that the Navajo, having banished the girl and her father, would be any more receptive to her return to Canyon de Chelly, regardless of her motives, than they would be to his own reappearance among them. In the second place, Carson's imported Ute raiders were notoriously sharp businessmen, with especial acumen in trading in flesh. A healthy Navajo woman would be farmed out at a good price as labor and convenience of some of the Spanish border ranchers up toward the Colorado valleys. But a captured white woman was worth a bale of prime beaver fur in ransom at any white post in the whole mountain country — and beaver was rapidly becoming a scarce commodity of trade. This always assuming the white woman's captors were of a mind to sell her.

He didn't like to think of the Spanish girl moving across country in which the Utes had officially been invited to hunt.

TEN

Twenty minutes after his break from Carson's camp Lindquist managed to check the frightened horse he was riding and quiet the animal. Without saddle, bridle, or surcingle, he had little control. And once into the network of the Navajo canyons, a horse would be completely useless anyway. Unburdened, the animal veered back toward the mesa top. Its clattering faded, and night silence clamped down tightly again.

Lindquist climbed carefully to the crest of a sandstone spine which appeared to point like a finger into the empty darkness which lay over the void of Canyon de Chelly. There was good footing atop this and less chance of a sudden drop into space than there was if he followed one of the dry watercourses which rutted the mesa rim. Besides, he wanted a vantage point from which he could locate himself and determine a way to reach the nearest of the Navajo as soon as daylight permitted. The Indians were due at least a warning of the presence of the Utes and the outline of the orders under which

124

Pfieffer and Captain Carey were operating. And Micaela might reach Chief Juanito's people during the night. Through them he might locate her.

Cold wind began to come out of the dark on either side the spine Lindquist was traveling, and the rock narrowed abruptly. He hoped he had picked one of the promontories of harder stone which had resisted the wash of wind and water here and there to jut far out into the main courses of the Navajo canyons. If so, its view should be commanding in daylight and he should be able to build a line of movement from it.

The updraft on either side of him became more pronounced. The stone underfoot cracked with fissures and was covered with treacherous loose rock, indicating he was near the disintegrating end of the promontory. It seemed likely he had gone far enough in the darkness and he hunkered down. Driven by the upsweeping wind, night chill bit into him, attacking at the tail of his jacket, his collar, and his wrists. A mildly miserable discomfort, against which there was no defense as long as he remained where he was. Lindquist grinned a little and wondered at his own humor. Sleep usually improved a man's disposition. Hunkering in the open in the small hours of the morning should not.

From himself he turned to thinking of Micaela and her bolt from Carson's camp. He was still thinking of her, a little warmed by private considerations and the chill of the night forgotten, when red light began to rise faintly in the east and the detail of his immediate surroundings began to grow recognizable.

Perhaps thirty yards away the promontory broke into the sheer edge he had sensed in the darkness, an edge overhanging the vastness of Canyon de Chelly. Near the edge, almost like a stone survey marker, a pylon of weathered rock jutted up. Seated against this, a man was huddled against the dawn cold, but awake and alert, nevertheless. Lindquist spotted him first as a shadow which might be a part of the upright rock itself. By the time he knew the shadow was a man and a cavalryman, the light had grown strong enough for any movement of his own to draw attention. Since he could not withdraw without detection, he did the next best thing. Studying the promontory farther back toward the mesa and the draws on both sides, he located the man's horse, hidden with reasonable caution in a clump of brush. There was only the one horse and no evidence of further cavalrymen in the vicinity. Lindquist shrugged slightly. One-to-one odds were more than a man could usually expect.

Light grew stronger. The man beside the upright rock did not look back along the spine connecting his position with the main body of the mesa, and there seemed no point in further waiting. Lindquist drew a belt gun and cocked it. The Army Issue weapon had twice the sear tension Lindquist liked and it clicked loudly as the hammer came into position. The man beside the rock pivoted sharply at the sound. Lindquist held the muzzle of the gun steadily on him.

"Easy, now, Steve . . ." he said, friendly and firm.

The quick tension of surprise slid away from Steve Grayson. He scowled, annoyance sharp in his manner. He raised his voice the slight edge above conversational tone necessary to bridge the distance between them.

"Damn you, Rick!" he growled. He started to rise.

Lindquist made a very plain motion with the gun. "I said easy, Steve!" he warned. "I'll do the moving. You sit tight!"

Grayson blinked uncomprehendingly,

but he settled slowly back, his eyes fixed more on the gun than on Lindquist. He was a brighter soldier than most. He understood the gun's warning, even when it didn't make sense to him. A lot of young bluecoats had to get themselves shot before they caught onto what a gun lined at their bright brass belt buckle might mean. It was a kind of hard way to learn a lesson. Lindquist was glad Steve Grayson didn't need any such teaching — this morning at least.

Rising, he began to work along the spine, keeping himself low enough to avoid distant silhouette in the thin dawnlight, until he reached the rock against which Grayson was leaning. Grayson tilted his nose at Rick's gun as though he was halfway between having his feelings hurt and being downright angry.

"What the hell kind of business is this?" he protested.

Lindquist felt philosophical. He figured he might as well share the feeling. It might be a long time till breakfast for either Grayson or himself.

"First law of the mountains," he said pleasantly. "Self-preservation. You spotted up here as lookout for Pfieffer?"

"No," Grayson grunted sourly. "I'm

looking for eggs of the night-flying ibis to go with my issue bacon!"

Lindquist let this go. A lot of men were pretty grouched the first hour after sunrise. He waggled his gun.

"What signals have you got rigged up with Pfieffer?"

Grayson's scowl darkened. "Confound it, Rick, put that iron up!"

Lindquist waggled the gun again, very insistently. Grayson studied his face and his eyes widened.

"We were talking about the signals you've got rigged with Captain Pfieffer, Steve," Lindquist prompted gently.

Grayson nodded and wet his lips. "Usual ones. Right and left arms for right and left. Both arms high for up, down for down. You know."

"Yeah," Lindquist agreed. He hunched along the stone under him till the upright rock was between him and the upper courses of the yawning canyon. Grayson hunched around a little, too, to make talking easier.

"Spotted here to steer Pfieffer through that broken country yonder, eh?" Lindquist asked.

Grayson grinned a little. "My idea. Not bad, eh? Down in these breaks yesterday afternoon we couldn't see a thing. Hit one blind run after another and had to keep turning back. So I climbed up here. Captain Pfieffer can put a glass on me, and every time I see the detachment stop, I can signal them which way to turn next. Save the rest of 'em a lot of time and me a lot of saddle sores."

"Smart," Lindquist agreed with approval. "Convenient, too. Suppose Pfieffer could pick me out with his glass where I'm sitting now?"

Grayson glanced at Lindquist and then off up the canyon, frowning in estimate. Finally he shook his head.

"No, 'fraid not. You'll have to move over this way a little more. I can see the column. Ranks broken for breakfast. Be moving again directly."

Lindquist sighed contentedly and carefully remained where he was.

"Hope they eat hearty," he said. "They're in for a hell of a ride."

"I don't get that, Rick," Grayson said uneasily.

Lindquist smiled, all friendliness, at him. "You will," he said.

He put his gun convenient to his hand on the rock and stretched with the luxuriance of a man anticipating a well-earned period of leisure. Grayson's unease became full disapproval.

"You being here doesn't make sense, Rick."

"Does to me."

"Colonel Carson didn't say so, but I got the definite impression you were more or less under arrest back at camp when we pulled out."

"Guess I was — more or less."

"Then what are you doing here?"

"Getting ready to make fools out of your detachment — with your help, of course."

Grayson stiffened and belatedly became very military.

"Over my dead body!"

Lindquist picked up his gun and looked at it. He smiled.

"It might come to that," he agreed. His smile widened. "Hardly likely, though. You got a head on your shoulders, Steve. You're a pretty smart boy. Too smart to buck at fate. This just isn't your day. Fortunes of war and all —"

Grayson did have a head on his shoulders. He subsided. Presently he raised a glass which had been lying on the rock on the other side of him and focused it on the maze of cuts and tributaries which formed a labyrinth about the true course of the

131

canyon below them. Lindquist squinted in the same direction and presently located Pfieffer's distant force. He chuckled.

"Hell of a note, isn't it? They can't get down into the canyon until they trace its course upstream to where the walls break down. And when they're in those cuts down there, they can't tell which one keeps them close to the main course of the canyon at all. Why, they might take a week making ten miles in those breaks!"

Grayson lowered the glass but said nothing. Lindquist pointed toward the distant column.

"They're signaling for directions, I reckon. Give them the sign, Steve. Start them up that gorge that's in shadow — to the left of where they are now. The one with the black streak under the cap rock."

Grayson sucked in a breath.

"Now listen, Rick! That'll take 'em clear back up to the mesa rim, way back up in that malpais. They'll lose half a day or more. You can see that from here."

"Sure can," Lindquist agreed. "But they can't see it from where they are. That's what I like. Make your signal."

Grayson stood up and after a moment sullenly began swinging his arms in a double circle for attention. Lindquist leaned over and picked up the officer's glass. It halved the apparent distance to Pfieffer's command, making even individuals discernible.

"They're watching you," he said.

Grayson glanced at Lindquist, then shrugged helplessly, braced himself, and started to make his signals. Lindquist swiftly put down the glass and cocked his gun. Grayson looked at the weapon. He lost a kind of wild look in his eyes and lowered his partially raised right hand. Lifting his left arm, he swung it to indicate the distant side canyon under the black streak of cap rock. Asking for the glass, he watched Pfieffer's detachment for a moment, then repeated the signal with clarifications. Eyes unaided were enough for Lindquist to determine that Captain Pfieffer was accepting the directions he had dictated. He let down the hammer on the gun and smiled at Steve Grayson.

"Rest your hocks," he suggested. "Sit down. We got a bit of traveling to do ourselves, directly. Save up for it."

"Traveling?"

"Sure. We can't keep Pfieffer out of the main canyon forever. He'll get wise to you. Next thing now is to let the Navajo know he's coming in time for them to clear out ahead of him."

"Warn the Navajo?" Grayson whitened with the shock his neatly tailored military man's code suffered at this. "Rick, you're crazy! This is going too far. I'm going to —"

"You're going to be agreeable or you're going to be sort of dead, Steve," Lindquist cut in. "I thought I made that plain."

There was bite to the words, Lindquist's earlier humor lifting like a curtain to reveal iron beneath. Grayson came smack up against this, and the impact hurt. He subsided again. But his outrage needed some vent.

"Murderers!" he said quietly. "Killers! And you're going to warn them!"

"Your uniform says that's what you are — and a professional, to boot. A hired killer. So are the boys we just sent on a long ride. So's Carson."

"We're soldiers, with legal authority!" Grayson snapped. "We're fighting for the law. There's a difference."

"Sure is," Lindquist admitted. "The Navajo are fighting for their homes — more than that — for their Washington, D.C., their Bunker Hill and Lexington and Concord. For their Plymouth Rock and Boston Harbor and Old Virginia. That's what's in these canyons!"

It was pretty and about as earnest as a man could be. Maybe so pretty that another time Rick Lindquist would have been a little ashamed of decking out something important so fancy. But for the moment he was right proud he'd hit the right words to bring a feeling out where another man could see it. Grayson didn't seem to see too well, however. He spat.

"There's a bunch of brush huts and some busted-down old mud buildings and some dusty caves in these canyons. That and a bunch of savages who've broken the law —" Intensity shook his voice. "I've got no use for a man that turns against his own kind!"

"Neither have I," Lindquist said. "Leastways, without plenty of provoking. Point is, I guess I see these — these savages a little different than you."

Grayson swore, perhaps because he could think of nothing more to say, perhaps because he had said too much already. He glared at Lindquist. Rick waited him out, knowing what was coming. The Army sent a lot of greenhorns and occasionally a fool out across the Missouri, but it seldom sent a coward. After a long time Grayson indicated Lindquist's gun and patted the flapped holster at his own belt.

"I've got a sidearm too, Rick," he said. "You head for the Navajo and I'll use it on you the first chance I get."

"Maybe I better make you shuck it right now."

Grayson tensed. "Try it," he suggested.

Lindquist liked this. He grinned and shook his head.

"Later. Getting to the Navajo's only part of the chore ahead of us."

"Yeah?" Grayson was wary.

"I had to kill a sentry in camp last night, getting away."

"Expect me to be surprised?" Grayson snapped. "You didn't think you'd find our sentries sleeping in hostile country, did you?"

"It was me that was surprised. This wasn't a trooper. He was a Ute — in full paint."

"A Ute — down here?"

Grayson's incredulity reflected to his credit how much he had learned of this country in the brief tour of this expedition. He was a good man.

"Carson had a tentful of them, laying out some kind of a plan. This one was watching the Ute horses when he got in my way. Carson and the Army are turning those mountain devils loose on the Navajo."

Grayson considered this gravely. He seemed doubtful for a moment, but the set of Lindquist's features seemed to convince him he heard the truth. He shook his head slowly.

"Sounds more like an order from department headquarters — or Washington." He shook his head again. "It couldn't be Colonel Carson."

"They were in Kit's tent."

"So what do you want me to do — help drive the Utes off?"

"The two of us may wish we'd tried just that before we're through," Lindquist agreed. "The Castaneda girl slipped out of camp sometime before I made my break. Carson discovered she was missing and figured I had her with me. Probably saved me from getting my hide ventilated by your blasted troopers. They sure opened up on my tail before Carson called them off."

Grayson frowned heavily, then shrugged. "She knows the country. She'll get to the Navajo. She'll be all right."

"I'm not so sure about the Navajo — even if she does get to them. But if she doesn't — if she runs into some of the Utes instead . . ."

"You think there's a chance they might pick her up?"

Lindquist nodded soberly. "A big chance."

"How do we find out?"

"Locate the Navajo and see if she reached them."

Grayson closed his eyes for a moment and breathed heavily. When he opened them he nodded at Lindquist's gun.

"Put it away, Rick. You won't need it. Captain Pfieffer has sixty men with him. He can take care of himself for a few hours. But that girl's alone. It looks like I'm going Navajo hunting with you."

"Don't take it so hard, having to give up your detachment," Lindquist offered in dry comfort. "Didn't somebody write something once about women playing hell with war —" He paused significantly. "Or was it soldiers? I don't remember."

"The hell you don't!" Grayson said with feeling.

Lindquist grinned. There was something a little incredulous in anything but trail talk and mountain lore and tales of big drunks coming out of a man in buckskin. It always upset a newcomer to encounter some shine of civilization which had not been completely tarnished over by hard and solitary living. Grayson was no exception.

Rick picked up Grayson's glass and focused it up the canyon. He watched for a long moment till a notch in the broken country revealed Pfieffer's command patiently filing up the blind side canyon under the black cap rock. He stood up.

"Might as well haul breeches," he said. "Your soldier boys won't be in the big canyon today. That's for sure."

Grayson heaved to his feet, and they started back along the rock spur toward the body of the mesa. Lindquist moved in the lead, calmly trusting Grayson behind him, knowing he could do so with impunity. Something vaguely troubled him about this, and he finally identified the unfamiliar twinge as a sort of rudimentary conscience.

He had deliberately baited Grayson with the information about the Spanish girl. Not because of a need for help in what might lie ahead — actually, he would have preferred to work alone — but because he could not leave Grayson at liberty to return to headquarters with word of his own whereabouts and intent.

Grayson was with him because of the girl, and there was a certain dishonesty in

this because Eric Lindquist had no intention of permitting the young lieutenant to
interfere with an increasingly pleasant bit
of thinking growing in his mind. Thinking
which involved reappraisal of himself as a
man of certain charm and desirability, with
consideration of Micaela Castaneda as its
object.

ELEVEN

Once back onto the mesa proper, they paused long enough to free Grayson's horse of saddle and gear and turn the animal loose, then started along parallel to the rim, watching for some sign of the foot trail Micaela had said existed somewhere along this south wall in the middle reaches of the canyon. The side slopes and the floor of the chasm, of which they had occasional glimpses, were still in night shadow — dark patches reaching across the red splendor of the general formation and constantly changing as the sun rose higher. As they moved Grayson betrayed that he, too, thought of the Spanish girl.

"You know, Rick, something puzzles me to beat the devil," he said slowly. "I can understand the Indians coming to a place like this. It's a natural fortress. A place they can hold. There's water, graze, good enough land to grow the thin crops they need. But old man Castaneda, for instance. His kind is used to good living. You can see that. Neighbors, lamplight, rich tables, dancing and music. This is no place for him."

"Or the girl?"

141

"Especially her, Rick."

"How'd you turn out to be a soldier, Steve?" Lindquist asked him.

Grayson looked a little surprised and somewhat defensive. "Because I liked soldiering, I guess. The excitement you hit sometimes. The country you see . . ."

"Now you've got it. The country — that's it."

Grayson made an impatient gesture. "Sure — sure, the country! The good of your soul and all. Room, emptiness, challenge. I get that. But that's all just words when it comes to settling down in a place — putting up a house — admitting this is as far as you're going. Beans and bacon are what become important then. A man's got to have more than that. So does a woman."

Lindquist shrugged. "Maybe. Down on the benches in these canyons the Navajo have some of the finest crop patches you've ever seen, Steve. The Castanedas had some beautiful fields at their place. I saw them. And the benches that weren't fenced were rich with grass. I've been thinking about it. If a man wanted to run stock, this would make a fine place for a ranch."

"You think that's what brought Castaneda in here — a stock ranch?"

"Most Spanish-Americans are stockmen, one way or another. A rancher can build himself up to a pretty fine living, Steve. He can be his own king. That makes up for a lot of things."

Grayson stopped and looked quizzically at his companion.

"You're talking this mighty pretty, Rick. You aiming to turn rancher — you?" He stopped and laughed at the incredulity of the thought. "Rick Lindquist — mountain man, scout, trapper — with a farmer's dirt under his fingernails? Hell, the first time you found yourself inside of a fence you'd head for the tall timber!"

"Once, maybe," Lindquist agreed. "Now, I don't know. The timber doesn't grow tall any more, Steve. The biggest sticks have been cut. There isn't a place a man can go and hope to find the old days. Days you never saw. Wagons are raising dust from the Plattes to the Columbia. There are railroads clean out to the Missouri. The best of the fur's gone, and the men who made the Trade the thing it used to be are gone with it. Jim Bridger's holed up with rheumatism in his fort on the Snake. Dick Wooten's running a toll road over Raton Pass. Indians have killed Charlie Bent and Old Bill Williams. Carson's turned guide for Frémont and your Army. Where does that all leave me?"

"All right. Turn stockman, then. But why here?"

"It's a smarter idea than you think. Seasons are sort of backward in this country, leastways as far as stock is concerned. Summers run hot enough to burn up the grass. There's summer rain, but the runoff's so fast there's few places stock can water during the hot months on top of the mesas. Come winter, forage freshens and there's water. Timber gives shelter from the worst storms too. Stock does good on mesas in the winter."

"That's just half your year."

"That's where the deep canyons come in. They're cooler than the mesas and shaded from the sun in summer. There's good summer forage on the benches scattered through them. A five-foot well dug through the sand will bring in good water anywhere along a canyon floor the driest day of the year. Graze the canyons in summer and the mesas in winter and you'd have fat beef to sell the Army quartermaster."

"You been giving this some thought!" Grayson grunted. "I near believe you're serious!"

"Figure I might be, at that," Lindquist agreed.

Grayson shot him a sidelong glance. "A man don't ranch alone, Rick. Stock raising means settling permanently. Fencing — buildings — a house — a wife, even."

"Yeah," Lindquist conceded. "Be convenient, all right. Especially that last."

Grayson swung around to face him squarely.

"Listen, you Scandinavian procrastinator! All this isn't by chance a way of telling me you've got an eye on that girl, is it?"

Grayson was obviously suffering at the thought. Lindquist enjoyed that. A man liked to have a stronger carcass than the next. He liked to know more about the business at hand. He liked to shoot straighter. And there was something universal in an Indian's delight over the theft of a woman from another. He shrugged elaborately.

"It's a hell of a long ride to another suitable female, Steve," he pointed out.

"Suitable!" Grayson exploded. "Why, you stinking old mountain goat! Before I'd let that girl be forced to live the rest of her life with — with a half savage like you, I'd — I'd —"

"What, for instance?"

Grayson looked helplessly about. "It's — it's ridiculous! Utterly ridiculous! Come on, we're wasting time!"

He strode rapidly away. Lindquist followed him. The satisfaction was gone. He didn't like the word Grayson had used — ridiculous. Maybe because it was in the back of his own mind — had been, all along. Maybe it was because it was too close to the truth.

He had been letting his mind do a little experimenting. He had gotten over his first acute discomfort with Micaela, both in actual presence and in speculation. In a mental extension of their relationship he had encountered no difficulty in the prospect of workaday association — chores and the building up of something together — mealtimes and the like. He could even envision an affection for him slowly growing in her.

But when there were shadows and lamplight and the great night loneliness of this country closed in on his speculative dreaming, he bogged down completely. There was no dreamed intimacy in which he could believe. Not with him. As Grayson said, it was ridiculous.

They had traversed perhaps two miles of

the canyon rim and Lindquist reckoned the sun still barely an hour high when they came across a dead Indian. He lay in a pocket of powdery soil washed into a small depression in the naked rock of the mesa rim from some distant hill by the great rains which occasionally swept this high desert. A starving ironwood bush had rooted in the thin soil, and its sparse growth partially hid the body.

Grayson dragged the dead man into the open. He was Navajo. He had been transfixed from behind by a heavy arrow bearing a broad-bladed iron trade point. And he had been scalped. Grayson rose from the body and crossed to Lindquist where he stood, a little apart. The lieutenant was all brisk efficiency, the way they taught men at Fort Leavenworth.

"Navajo," he said. "Killed since sunrise. Maybe half an hour ago. By another Indian. You can look at the arrow and probably identify it, but I'd say Ute without a question."

Lindquist nodded and pointed to the dust at his feet. It was trampled a little, disturbed, but there was a smooth patch of soft sand the size of a page from a book. In the center of this, impressed as neatly as a signature, was the single print of an excessively small Spanish boot. Grayson paled.

"Micaela!" he breathed.

Lindquist nodded again and with but a glance at the body of the dead Indian strode swiftly across the little pocket, looking for something he knew must be near. Grayson had to stretch his stride to keep up with him.

Two hundred yards away a deep, narrow gash was cut through the country rock of the mesa, slanting steeply downward as it approached the lip of the walls sheltering the main Navajo canyon. Lindquist spotted what he sought on the edge of this brief tributary and ran across to it. When Grayson came up he was down on one knee, fingering the first of a series of downward-staggered depressions in the otherwise smooth, steeply slanting wall of the crevice. He looked up at the young officer.

"No wonder she found that Navajo so quickly," he said. "She knew where this was — right where it was. And she must have come directly to it."

"To what?"

"This —" Lindquist indicated the depressions pocked into the rock. "The foot trail she told me about. That's what these are — hand and toe holds chipped out by the old cliff people."

Grayson looked carefully at the weathered depressions and shook his head.

"A goat couldn't get down those!"

"It isn't as hard as it looks."

"It couldn't be!" Grayson snorted. "Don't tell me Micaela climbed down that way into the canyon!"

"No. But this Navajo climbed up out of the canyon this way. Chief Juanito must have sent him to guard the head of this trail."

"You figure Micaela came up and started talking to him —"

"I think so," Lindquist agreed. "She was probably trying to get this sentry to let her past to see the chief. Probably had quite a job on her hands. When the Navajo ran her and her father out of the canyon, they made it plain the Castanedas weren't wanted back."

Grayson scowled and kicked the rock underfoot.

"The Utes must have been right behind her, then, Rick. While she had the sentry's attention, one of them let drive with that arrow. Then they grabbed her." Grayson's lips tightened. "Where would they take her, Rick?"

Lindquist paused before answering. He

tried to sort opinion from hope in his mind. It was an unpleasant task.

"Depends on the Utes, I reckon. How many of 'em, and so on. And just how ornery they're feeling. That horse sentry I killed last night in Carson's camp probably didn't improve their good nature. A white woman's first-class ransom bait, and they're ransom experts. If that's it, they'll start her back to their own villages as fast as they can. Over in the San Juans someplace. They'll hold her till the old man gets plenty worried and the Utes have got a couple ransom offers out of him. When they collect the best offer, they'll send her back."

"Unhurt?"

"Sure." Lindquist nodded without conviction. "Maybe needing a bath pretty bad. That's all."

"But if they don't hold her for ransom?"

"Then I reckon they'd hide her around here someplace pretty close till they're done with whatever deviltry they cook up for her."

Grayson took off his hat and poked his fingers through his hair. He looked expectantly at Lindquist, as though for reassurance. There was none. Finally he put his look into words.

"What's her chances, Rick? Are the Utes really bad medicine?"

Lindquist shrugged. "The worst kind — to the Navajo. They're enemies. Always have been. When it comes to whites, I don't know. Utes have as much reason as most of the others to hate us. Maybe more. But Chief Ouray's held them at peace with us for quite a spell — officially, at least. The Army's used a lot of them for scouts. Guess it boils down to there being good Utes and bad Utes, same as anybody else."

"But you don't know," Grayson prodded tautly.

"Nobody does," Lindquist answered patiently. "How can they know, when there's a woman involved? You couldn't even tell about your own troopers in the same situation."

"Yeah," Grayson agreed heavily. "I sure couldn't — not this long out of headquarters!"

He turned to look back over the mesa. A pinnacle of rock tilted into a rise in middle distance, poking high above the timbered evenness of the mesa crown. He pointed to it.

"We can hit that peak in a couple of hours, Rick. This glass of mine is a good one. They can't have too much of a start.

Maybe we can pick them up with it. It's our best chance."

"If we located them — then what?"

Grayson's eyes brightened with the relief of shaping plans. His voice quickened eagerly, as though the girl's rescue was imminent.

"You're good at trailing. You could light out after them while I headed for Captain Pfieffer's detachment. You could keep under cover, make sure she didn't get hurt, till I got back with the troop. Tomorrow at the latest. Won't be any trouble making the Utes give her up to uniforms. They're supposed to be working for the Army here."

"Tomorrow," Lindquist said softly. He knelt to look again at the toe holds in the crevice before them.

Anger rose visibly in Grayson. "One thing's sure," he grunted. "The Utes didn't climb down into the canyon with her. Get off your hunkers. We're losing time!"

"I know. And we've got to lose more, Steve. We've got to go down to the floor of the canyon first — Utes or no Utes."

"We *what?*" Grayson exploded. "Doesn't that make sense!"

"Not much. But I told you I had to get to the Navajo first and then to the girl. That's the way it still is."

"What's the matter with you, Lindquist? Don't you realize what may happen to Micaela?"

Lindquist's mouth was dry. He didn't need Grayson's abrupt dropping of his first name for his last. He knew what he was saying, what he was doing. He felt as though the breakfast he had not eaten had poisoned him. He had seen animals in a trap suddenly erupt in a fury unaccountable either by fear or what pain they suffered. Their frenzy had always mildly puzzled him. Animals were practical, and such outbursts were not practical. But he understood them now. He knew the feeling which accompanied them. It was not the trap or the trapper or a fear of death they fought, but the utter helplessness of their position. And Lindquist was caught now.

He wheeled on Grayson. The young officer saw his expression and backed involuntarily. Lindquist's voice shook, although he fought to keep it from rising.

"You stiff-necked young idiot! How many years have you been in the mountains? I know more about Indians than you will ever hear. I know more about the things they can think up to do than you could dream up with a fever, whiskey, and a bilious belly! I'm not telling you what I

153

want to do. I'm telling you what we've got to do. Get started down those handholds!"

Grayson backed another step. He made no attempt to hide his utter disgust. He made no attempt to hide the surge of righteous defiance sweeping him.

"No," he said. "You'd better not, either. Once I've found Micaela, Lindquist, I'll hunt you down. You warn the Navajo and I'll kill you!"

Lindquist's fury still shook him. "Try it now," he begged harshly. "You and your Army suit! A little tin god going after her. Where the hell's your armor and your white horse? Try something, damn you. Try anything!"

He started forward, his movements barely under physical control, his hands wanting something for an instant that they could crush. His head was forward, his shoulders hunched, his eyes rigidly steady. He wanted violence. He wanted release.

Grayson backed another step, staring at him with a condemnation more forceful than a blow. Suddenly the lieutenant spun on his heel and trotted away — back toward the body of the mesa, toward the distant pinnacle of rock from which he hoped to locate the girl and her captors. And he did not look back, although the certainty of death must have been very close to him.

Lindquist watched him go, standing bent a little and tense, until the fury ran from him and he was empty. Reason returned slowly. He could not have gone with Grayson. Grayson could not go with him. He believed it was Grayson who was right.

Decency was a large thing, made up of many threads. It was a heritage of family and association, of things remembered and things forgotten. It was fragile and would fray under hard usage. The safety of Micaela Castaneda was the thing decency made paramount here. And he had set warning the Navajo ahead of it. Maybe it was that he had been too long in the mountains, and mountain men forgot what decency they had once known as they forgot how to wear any other clothing than the greasy leather gear of their trade.

However it was, Lindquist turned slowly, knelt, and started down the handholds in the crevice before him, working his way feet first, with his face turned to the red sandstone of de Chelly.

TWELVE

Every time she shut her eyes Micaela could see again the bloody war arrow erupt from the breast of the Navajo sentry as she stood talking to him in the cold half-light of dawn. She could see the expression of anguished surprise and swift death which wiped it away. She could feel the impact of his body as it fell against her and smell the strong, sickish scent of fresh blood pumping in quantity over her. She could see the two Utes rising from the brush which had concealed them.

When she opened her eyes she could still see them. One on either side, urging her ever higher up one of the brush-choked ravines which scarred the mesa top. Big men. Arrogantly handsome. Acquisitive. Obviously on the hunt and vain of their quarry. More predatory than the Navajo. More savage.

She had not been frightened at first. She had seen the Ute chiefs arrive at Carson's camp. She knew what their presence meant. She had been trying to get a warning to Chief Juanito when these two surprised her at the head of the foot trail.

For a time she had believed her captors would return her to Colonel Carson's camp, since they were in Army employ. But it became increasingly apparent they had something else in mind. The ravine they traveled led in the wrong direction. The two of them were too gleeful of their captive, too warily cautious of each other. And although she fought strongly against it, knowing it robbed her of what little defense she might have, she could feel the increasing rise of a massive terror.

The Utes stopped beneath an overhang in one portion of the ravine wall. The ground was level and dry beneath it. Smoke stain against the red rock indicated it had served as shelter before. One of the Utes seemed satisfied with the place. The other was not. They harangued in their own tongue, and the harangue became an open quarrel. At length the one who had chosen this place subsided and the other motioned her on again, taking by virtue of his victory a slightly more proprietary air with her.

She struggled through a brush thicket and into a slot where the ravine narrowed. It was dark, a forbidding place. The proprietary Ute gripped her arm. She thought he grinned. At the upper end of the slot a great hollow had flaked out of the ravine wall, leaving a heap of broken rock on the floor, partially closing the hollow and leaving what amounted to a cave. Within this was a rock-and-rubble structure, mortared with mud and plastered, but long roofless. It was one of the ruins of the ancients — half a dozen cramped rooms with low, interconnecting doorways. Micaela thought it belonged to the time of the Basket Makers, the forgotten ones who had been in de Chelly before the first of the great pueblo builders.

The cramped rooms looked ugly, evil, suffocating. There was an old and ugly feeling in the ravine. There was an old and ugly thing in the eyes of the Utes. Micaela trembled. She was afraid. She was sick. She wanted to scream. She wondered why a woman always wanted to scream. A scream was not a weapon.

The Ute who had chosen the earlier shelter down the ravine recoiled when he saw the silent, dusty little building now ahead of them. Micaela had seen the fear in his eyes before and recognized it now, feeling a quick surge of hope.

There was a universal superstition which kept even the familiar Navajo from entering the old palaces of the dead except under the most compelling circumstances. She straightened and pointed at the little ruin and used the Navajo word for the spirits they believed lingered in these ancient places. It was doubtful either of her captors knew the Navajo word, but both appeared to understand its meaning. One drew back even farther from the entrance. The other spat an oath at him and struck at Micaela. When she reeled from the openhanded blow he seized her and thrust her violently through the doorway.

She fell on her knees within and scrambled hastily to her feet as the Indian started to follow her in. The other Ute seized this one in sharp protest. Their quarrel flamed again, anger up full in each of them. Understanding nothing of what they said, Micaela chose to believe they disagreed on the use of this forbidden place rather than over her. But she couldn't quite forget that wherever there were two men and a woman bad blood and violence seemed inevitable.

She backed a little and tripped over a stone half the size of her head. Her hand touched this as she caught herself and crouched against one crumbling wall of the ruin. The stone had a familiar feel, and she glanced down to see it was a *mano,* a patiently hand-shaped stone of the kind yet used by the Navajo women for grinding their corn in potholes in the mother rock of de Chelly.

The quarrel between the Utes seemed to ebb. The one without fear of the ancient spirits bent and came through the cave opening, his eyes on Michaela. She gripped the *mano* under her hand tightly. The Ute bent and caught her, lifting her up against him. But if it was an embrace, it was but half done. The second Ute leaped suddenly in from outside, a short, heavy knife in his hand. He landed upon the back of his companion. The knife struck. Micaela was crushed against the wall at her back by the two struggling bodies. She lost her footing and fell. Twisting, fighting desperately and silently, the two Utes rolled completely over her, driving her face into the sour old dust of the floor, bruising her against stone, driving the breath from her body.

Sobbing with hurt and the full grip of her terror, Micaela crawled aside. The Indian with the knife suddenly freed it and struck at the other with repeated fury. There was a cry and a fountain of blood, and the victorious Ute started to rise, watching the slow twisting of his victim's body warily.

Micaela's hand again found the ancient *mano*. She gripped it with both hands. It must have been heavy, yet it felt light. She raised it high. The Ute with the knife started to turn toward her. She brought the stone down with the full force of her fear behind it. The blow made little sound. The Ute shuddered and tilted slowly forward, spilling across the body of his companion. Micaela stared in the sudden silence at the man's head, misshapen by her blow with the old stone. With her hands to guide her and her legs unsteady beneath her, she made her way drunkenly along the walls of the cave to the entrance and so into the openness of the ravine, where the sun was.

But this was not enough. Her own breathing seemed to echo here. She suddenly and wildly wanted the wind against her face, the sky and space about her. She started recklessly to climb the opposite ravine wall. Part way up she paused and leaned across an outcropping. To rest, she thought, but actually to be suddenly and violently ill.

She retched an interminable time, then resumed her climb when strength returned. At the rim she came out on one of the open expanses of flat, bare rock which studded the timber and grass of the mesa

161

crown. In the center of this, moving diagonally away from her, was one of Colonel Carson's soldiers. So much relief flooded up in her that she choked up and tried twice before she could cry out:

"Señor!"

The soldier halted and spun warily about, startled. He saw her and began to run toward her. Micaela started to run also. Her knees buckled. The mesa top tilted crazily. She fell.

Having carried the girl across to the needle-carpeted shade of the nearest pines, Grayson put her down in the best form of accepted military practice. He put her down flat on her back, arms above the head to aid in breathing, his hat under her head to cushion it. She had obviously been in a violent struggle. Her clothing was awry and grimed with dust. So was her face. There was a great splash of drying blood on one sleeve of her blouse. And although her breathing seemed regular enough when he listened closely to it, she was incredibly pale.

Working carefully and with a delicacy which surprised him, he failed to locate a wound and realized the blood on her clothing must have come from someone else. Relieved, he sat back on his heels to watch her. Sun came through an aperture in the foliage overhead and struck highlights from her hair. Plastered with dust and disheveled, she was still beautiful. Small, but with a feeling of strength, he decided. He decided, also, that he liked women this way, although some of his warmest recollections were of women softer than this.

She was a kind of beautiful little animal. Grayson tried to visualize her in a gown at a post ball, moving from one tall uniform to another. She fitted.

He got to wondering if this wasn't really what he'd ridden a cavalry horse a thousand miles into the West for. Maybe this was really what he had been wanting when periods of restlessness came over him and his temper turned sour and he disliked everything about his surroundings — himself most of all.

A man needed a woman. That was a fact. He could forget women for long months on end. He could work his way through a tour of duty, his mind wholly on service politics and the prospect of getting himself raised a grade in rank. Then suddenly, without warning, there he was thinking of women — of the best he had known and the worst, and not being too fussy about it, at that. When this happened, a woman became more important than anything else. Grayson scowled a little. It was a hell of a note and sometimes as inconvenient as the devil, but it was true.

He supposed the whole thing was love. There seemed little else to call it that was decent. And a man got over being too particular, too. West of the Missouri, allowances had to be made in most things. This was not a woman's country, and women were few.

Mountain men — trappers of Rick Lindquist's kind and even of Colonel Carson's — took companionship where they found it, to a large extent. It seemed to work out well enough, although it inevitably meant Indian women in some cases. There had been a time when Steve Grayson had been immensely incensed and disgusted by the so-called squaw men. He doubted he was so superior now. It was altogether blind, staggering luck that this girl was so proudly Spanish. Had she been Navajo or Ute, he was near certain the situation would have been the same. This was a woman he wanted.

She stirred presently. Her eyes opened and she looked at him. She closed them for a moment, then looked at him again. He thought she was trying to reassure herself that he actually existed. He smiled. She started to sit up. He leaned forward quickly to help her.

"All right now?" he asked.

She said something in Spanish, then nodded when she realized he had failed to understand her.

"The Utes had you — you got away from them?"

She nodded again.

"Are they still close?"

The girl shuddered. Her lips compressed as though she struggled to hold something down. Grayson glanced apprehensively about, aware with a guilty start that he had not been keeping efficient watch for her captors.

"They — they won't bother — now, Lieutenant," Micaela said unsteadily. She paused, and her mind quit this statement for another thought with a leap obvious to Grayson. "Are there more soldiers close?"

"At headquarters camp," he agreed. "And another detachment back in the malpais somewhere. Captain Pfieffer's men should be closer than those in camp. If you can travel, we ought to try finding Pfieffer."

"I've got to get into the canyon," Micaela said.

"You and your father were ordered out of it. You'll have to stay out."

"Didn't you ever disobey an order, Lieutenant?"

"Several times," Grayson agreed. "But you're not going to disobey this one. We're heading for higher ground to try to locate Captain Pfieffer. As soon as we straighten out the wrong signals Rick Lindquist made me give the captain . . ."

The girl's eyes brightened. "Rick?" she asked sharply. "I thought he was in the camp — a sort of prisoner."

"He escaped last night. Caught me short this morning and made a fool out of me."

"Where is he now?"

"Where you wanted to go — down into the canyon. And for the same reason, I think."

"The canyon?" Micaela paled a little. "They'll kill him down there!"

"The Navajo?" Grayson shook his head sourly. "I doubt that. He was taking them some useful information. If he has his way, he'll help them snarl up this whole campaign for the rest of us!"

"You don't understand!" Micaela protested. "The Navajo are frightened and angry. Rick helped lead your force in here in the first place. They won't believe anything he tells them. They may not even listen. He needs help quickly — someone who can talk to Juanito for him and make the chief listen!"

"Lindquist has earned whatever the Navajo may hand him by breaking out of camp last night," Grayson said stubbornly. "Those Indians are the enemy, and he took information to them."

"Does everybody have to wear a uniform just because you do?" Micaela snapped. "The Navajo aren't my enemies. If your Army had some regard for right, these Indians wouldn't be your enemies either! You've got to help me get back to the upper trail, quickly!"

She broke away. Grayson gripped her arm.

"Look, I found you," he protested. "You're with me now. How do I know those Indians wouldn't kill you if they got their hands on you? You're going with me!"

"That's brave talk, Lieutenant," Micaela said stiffly. "Can you back it up?"

Grayson didn't understand and grunted uncomprehendingly. Micaela indicated the ravine from which she had appeared.

"The two Utes — remember them? They were taking me someplace I didn't want to go. They're over there. And they're dead."

"Dead?" Grayson repeated incredulously. "You — ?"

Micaela nodded. "Dead," she agreed firmly.

Grayson grinned. "You wouldn't be trying to threaten me, would you?"

"I certainly am!"

"Thanks would be a little more in line. You weren't exactly in shape to go anyplace when I found you."

Micaela carefully scanned his face as though in measurement, then lowered her eyes.

"I'm sorry, Lieutenant," she murmured. "Rick Lindquist knows how I feel about the Navajo. I had a chance to talk with him. I don't want him harmed by them. But you make me ashamed. I do owe you a lot."

Grayson, encouraged and feeling on familiar ground again, moved closer to her.

"You sure do," he agreed easily. "And I could do with a little payment on account about now. . . ."

He pulled her into his arms. She made no protest, no evasion. Her head tilted upward. She looked again into his face with the openness of a little girl. A little girl who knew much of herself, of men, and the tides which might run between them. Grayson kissed her. She was responsive. Her lips were soft. It was good. Grayson drank deeply. He had anticipated rebuff, a measure of resistance. A period of conquest and some uncertainty. But this was better. In fact, it was wonderful. What was it Rick Lindquist had said about a suit of armor and a white horse? A man didn't need it. And Lindquist was a fool for his conviction this girl was his.

Grayson was delightedly well on his way to complete submergence in the eddies of this embrace when the girl stirred a little. A moment later something nudged him under the ribs. Micaela broke away from him. She stepped back a little, and he could see his own belt gun at full cock in her hand. Its muzzle was pressed with uncompromising firmness against his blouse.

Grayson swore inelegantly, angry and amused at the same time. He stood motionless for a moment, then snapped one hand downward to catch the gun and simultaneously took an easy, confident step forward. A dry stick in the needle carpeting under the pines caught his heel. Thrown off balance, he lunged with unintentional violence against the girl and his hand caught the barrel of the pistol rather than its hammer.

His weight knocked Micaela from her footing. They went heavily to the ground together, the gun somewhere between them. As they struck, the weapon fired. Grayson felt the heat of the muzzle flash. He could smell the strong acridity of burned powder. Rolling clear of the girl, he was conscious of no immediate pain. Rather it was a knowledge he had been hit and that pain would presently follow. An instant later numbness seemed to flow out from one side of his head to every fiber of his body. A numbness which submerged him completely, so that when he tried to protest what had happened, no sound issued from his throat. Nor could he move, after his first instinctive roll into the clear.

The girl rose slowly into his hazy field of vision. Her lips were trembling and her face was whiter than it had been when she collapsed before him on the edge of the ravine. He could feel blood — his life's blood — running generously down over one ear from some kind of great hole higher in his head. He knew Micaela stared at the wound. Her eyes were so stricken that he wanted to tell her it was all right.

He wanted to tell her it was all right and explore his wound with his fingers to determine the extent of damage. He wanted to hope it was only a crease, a glancing blow. He wanted to believe it wasn't much else. It couldn't be, unless death by a head wound did not come as he had always thought it did, in a single shattering instant.

Micaela bent over him for a moment, one hand touching the uninjured side of his head, fear in her eyes. Her breath caught in a kind of sob.

"Does — does it hurt?" she asked unsteadily.

Grayson tried to answer. He tried with everything in him to answer. But he lay helplessly in a paralysis. The girl straightened and looked helplessly about, then turned and ran beyond his narrowing range of vision. The bright morning sky was darkening. Grayson tried to follow her course. He thought she was running toward the big canyon, but he couldn't be sure. That was where Lindquist was — the big canyon. Certainly Micaela was running away from him. Maybe to Lindquist. Maybe the mountain man had been right, after all. Maybe the girl was his.

With this thought, the delayed hurt came

suddenly, like a rising wind. Grayson shut his eyes and fought the pain until it reached an agonizing crescendo. Oblivion rolled in then, blotting out the pain — blotting out everything — leaving nothing.

THIRTEEN

Micaela's foot trail into Canyon de Chelly was a fingernails-and-luck affair to Lindquist in spite of the fact that he had done a tolerable amount of rock climbing, one place and another. He supposed that when this weathered track had originally been pecked into the stone the steps had been much deeper and sharper and so provided surer footing. However, the storms of a thousand years had reduced the safety element, to say the least. He doubted if even the Navajo used this entry into their stronghold except in emergency.

He breathed more easily when he completed descent of the first sheer drop of the wall and reached a downward-slanting diagonal crevice which the original builders of the trail had utilized for a portion of the passage. This brought him swiftly closer to the floor of the canyon and forced him to a final consideration of the stand he would take with the Navajo when he reached them.

He was well aware of the difficulty he would face in convincing Juanito's people there was not some hidden trick in the warning he claimed to be delivering to them, some further purpose behind revealing to them the movements of the two cavalry detachments under Pfieffer and Carey. Indian devotion to logic often made the tribes most difficult to deal with, and there was little logic apparent in what he was trying to do.

His hope was to convince the people of de Chelly that he was sincerely opposed to Carson's planned campaign wholly on the basis of the justice involved. Whites before now — particularly men of the fur trade — had attempted to champion fair play for one tribe or another against the big companies, against opportunist members of their own kind, even against the Army and the Washington government. The Navajo would know this. So there was a precedent. They just *might* believe that Eric Lindquist was honestly opposed to the government's determination to chastise them and move them to Bosque Redondo. They just *might* believe he was their friend and listen to him because of this. They just *might* act upon his warning and advice. But it was expecting way too much of them to hope they would trust him. This they would not do and he knew it.

Whatever his beliefs and sympathies might be, he was still a white. By Indian logic, he would remain always a white, even should he change the color of his skin. They did not turn against their own kind within their tribal structure. They wouldn't believe that he'd turn against his own people. Whatever warning and information he brought them — however fully they acted upon it — he knew they would sharply guard against a trick on his part which would in the end bring final profit to the soldiers of the government.

History had already offered any Indian nation ample basis for distrust. It was the biggest handicap facing anyone who wanted to accomplish real and lasting good among any of the tribes. And occasionally it led to annihilation by the Indians of some of those who were their strongest and most sincere friends. The fact that there was a similar distrust of Indian motives among many of the settlers pouring across the Missouri did not make the job of the man who wanted to see a peaceful emigration any easier, either. This mutual wariness, in fact, seemed a more believable explanation for the increasing conflict along the frontier than any basis of cupidity among whites or savagery among the Indians.

On the last descent above the valley floor, Lindquist paused and looked up at the rim of de Chelly behind him. He wondered how long it would take to convince the Navajo of the truth of what he had to tell them, conceding he could even make them listen. Micaela was in grave trouble. He was sure of this. It was true that the Utes who had picked her up might return her immediately and without harm to Carson's camp. But Lindquist was inclined to apply his own reactions when in doubt over the probable movement of Indians. This was a young and beautiful woman by any standard, and a Ute would recognize this as readily as any other man. She might be held for ransom, as he had told Grayson, but Lindquist doubted it. Were he in the Utes' shoes he knew he would keep the girl. Guessing was that simple.

It seemed likely the Utes would attempt to hide her some distance from the point of her capture. This would take time. Micaela's life in de Chelly had made her familiar with Indian thinking and taboos. She would not make the errors of terror and hysteria which usually reduced white female captives to objects of disdain and abuse from the instant of capture. He believed that at worst she would be able to restrain even the Utes for a reasonable time by her natural arrogance. And she would be capable of some physical resistance.

The combination of these might gain enough delay. He hoped so. Certainly there was little chance Grayson, at a cavalryman's disadvantage when set afoot and knowing very little of the country or the kind of trail work confronting him, would find the girl.

Lindquist pitched on down the descent before him, moving as swiftly as the worn trail would permit, and frowning with helpless concern over Micaela. A last series of handholds let him down onto the sand of the canyon floor. As he stepped onto this, he heard a whisper of movement. He wheeled to face the charge of half a dozen Navajo who had all too obviously been patiently waiting for him to complete his downward climb. He made no sound, knowing nothing he said at this point would be listened to at all. And he made a show of keeping his hands away from the weapons at his belt. But neither did he stand still for capture. Among Indians a man won respect in one way, at least — a hard way, but usually convincing — by demonstrating just how much of a man he was. This was a language stronger than words.

He struck at the first of the Navajo, avoiding a face blow in shrewd deference to Indian aversion to the insult they universally felt was involved in the touch of another's hand to their face. He used hard, punishing body drives instead. Two of the Navajo went down, doubled agonizingly. But the rest crashed into him and bore him to the sand by weight of numbers. They mauled him and stripped his weapons. Thongs were produced. His wrists were lashed up into the small of his back. He was jerked to his feet and prodded reelingly across the canyon floor.

At the base of the north wall Lindquist was pushed onto a fissure which slanted up across the first lifting bulge of the barrier — the beginning of another foot trail similar to that by which he had descended the opposite wall of de Chelly. This fissure led to a narrow ledge perhaps a hundred feet above the canyon floor. His captors turned him back along this to a kind of steep ravine or chimney which reached dizzyingly upward. Traversing this, they came out at the base of a sheer rise but a few degrees from perpendicular. Spotted up across this bald cliff face was another series of the little pockmarked toe holds which had served the ancients for stairs.

A Navajo shoved past Lindquist and climbed swiftly by means of these. With the Indian ahead to demonstrate how to place his feet so that his movement matched the spacing of the weathered notches in the rock, Lindquist was able to climb with less difficulty than he anticipated.

It was nevertheless a steep, taxing climb from which a man did not want to look downward. Even if he kept his eyes on the rock facing in front of his nose, there was no way to avoid the sickening sensation of climbing in air alone. An awareness that a misstep meant an agonizingly long fall to certain death. Lindquist's muscles had tensed almost to a point of awkwardness when the Navajo ahead of him disappeared. A moment later his own head came up over a low masonry parapet and he sprawled onto a shelf or bench nearly an acre in extent. Above this the farther wall of the canyon hung in a great, outward-curving canopy of protection.

A mound of rubble against the base of this curving wall indicated this shelf had also once held an ancient city. But openness to the weather or falling stone from above had destroyed it.

Perhaps forty grim-faced Navajo men were on the shelf. Among them was Chief Juanito. Lindquist's captors prodded him forward. A long harangue began among the Navajo. Listening to it, aware he was its subject, but powerless to understand fully all he heard, Lindquist judged this particular location was serving as a sort of command post for the widely deployed Navajo force.

There were a number of younger men gathered a little apart. Many of them wore buckskin knee pads, which puzzled him until he realized such protection would be of great aid in climbing the old trails and the slick red rocks of the canyon walls. This group carried no weapons beyond their knives. It seemed likely they were couriers, held in readiness for any messages which must go out.

The others were older men, the very old, for the most part — too old to be effective warriors. A chief's council was often composed of such veterans as these.

When Lindquist's escort completed its report of his capture, each man giving his version with considerable gestures and all of the enthusiasm of a victorious skirmish at the beginning of a very uncertain campaign, Juanito withdrew and spoke at length with the older men. When the chief returned to face his prisoner, Lindquist had the feeling he had already been tried and judged. It was a feeling which made a poor substitute for breakfast.

Juanito eyed him a long moment in silence, then spoke for the first time in Spanish.

"The soldiers sent you," he accused with the flatness of conviction.

"Do I wear a uniform?" Lindquist countered. "The soldiers are looking for me as they look for Juanito and the Navajo. Because of me part of them are climbing blind side canyons onto the mesa instead of climbing down into de Chelly itself."

Juanito considered this gravely. He glanced at the group of older men. Lindquist gathered they all knew of Pfieffer's wild-goose chase and his explanation of it interested them. However, this was sheer guessing. No signal he could see passed between the chief and the elders. Juanito turned back to him.

"You lie," he said calmly. "All whites lie."

Lindquist nodded with what he hoped was disarming honesty.

"A good part of the time, I reckon," he agreed. "Particularly in dealing with Indians. But usually only to save their skins, one way or another."

Juanito smiled, seemingly pleased with this corroboration, if not with its qualification.

"But not me," Lindquist went on. "Not this time. When I climbed back into your canyon I knew you'd grab me. I didn't figure my skin was worth very much. I don't now. Why should I try lying to save it?"

Juanito considered this, also, again turning to the older men. They knotted a little more closely together, exchanging looks among themselves, but again there was no apparent interchange of signal with the chief. But when Juanito again faced Lindquist, he launched into a series of terse, shrewd questions which effectively broke up any continuity the story his prisoner had to tell might otherwise have. Such questioning would have reduced a carefully rehearsed alibi to a shambles of contradiction and confusion.

Lindquist answered only what was asked, as briefly as possible, but in five minutes Juanito knew the full story of his break from Carson's camp, his meeting with Steve Grayson, and the false signals which had sent Pfieffer's detachment climbing blindly into the malpais. All that was withheld was the fact the Castaneda girl had also escaped Carson's camp and was apparently now in the hands of some Ute raiders somewhere on the south mesa. It was unlikely this information would interest the Navajo, since they had run the girl and her father out of the canyon, and Lindquist was anxious that there be no uncertainty among the Navajo as to his motives in what he had done. It was best to leave Micaela completely out of it for now.

When Lindquist finished, Juanito ordered his hands untied and food brought for him. He sat down to munch on a couple of thin cakes of *mano*-ground corn meal pounded into a shredded jerky of venison and heavily leavened with Spanish pepper before baking on a flat rock. A portion of stone grit and wood ash and a strong flavor of wood ash and smoldering sheep dung were also among the ingredients. Lindquist had tasted better fare and worse, and the cakes sat well enough on his stomach. He felt better for having eaten.

His head, nursed well along toward healing by Micaela before abandonment of the Castaneda *estancia*, throbbed a little now. He examined the scar with his fingers while he waited for Juanito to have done talking with the older men. A Navajo presently approached him and signaled for him to join the Council. He rose and crossed stiffly. There was no friendliness yet discernible on the faces facing him. He started to sit down. The Indian who had summoned him caught his arm sharply to prevent him from doing this.

"Members of the Council sit," Juanito growled severely. "The chief sits. You stand!"

Well aware of the personal dignity prized among all of the tribes, among others as well as themselves, Lindquist jerked his arm away from the Navajo beside him and blandly disobeyed the chief's order, hunkering down comfortably with apparently complete assurance.

"Friends sit at a Navajo council also," he said quietly.

Several of the older men stirred and Juanito scowled, but he tilted his head in dismissal and the Indian near Lindquist moved away. Rick drew a deep breath. For the first time since he had climbed onto this ledge he felt he could afford to breathe. He realized he had presented the Navajo with something he didn't quite understand. But he had made headway. He had gained a hearing. Until they were sure of him now, they would make no disposition of the problem he presented. He grinned at the members of the Council as though confident and content.

"You call yourself friend," Juanito growled. "A man does not give his friendship to his enemy for nothing!"

"True," Lindquist conceded. "There's a price on mine, all right."

"What?"

Lindquist withheld his answer for a moment. It was not so much a matter of how to say it as it was to be sure of the answer himself. It was a matter of being absolutely certain of what he wanted to say and why he wanted to say it.

"The soldiers," he proposed quietly. "Let the soldiers go — let them get out of here before you have a war on your hands."

Juanito's features slackened a little in bafflement.

"Let the soldiers go?" he repeated. "What foolishness is this? Did we bring the soldiers here? Are they our prisoners? Do we want them? Are we keeping them? You make crazy talk!"

"I make good talk."

"Ah!" the Navajo snorted. "If there are

prisoners in de Chelly, it is the Navajo who are prisoners!"

"Maybe that can be changed," Lindquist suggested. "Changed a little, at least. Enough to make the soldiers give up. But if they do give up, I want your promise you'll let them go. I want the promise of all of your people this time too. A few of your young men began all this trouble out in the Rio Grande Valley. I want to know you can control them now."

The Indian chief stiffened. His hand swept the circle of older men facing Lindquist.

"This is the Council. I am chief. Our people are here. . . ." He cupped his two hands as though he held the whole Navajo nation in the hollow thus formed. "Their lives are here. Their land is here. We are to protect them from the enemy. So long as we do this, we control them. Without protection, they fight for themselves. There is no control then."

Juanito paused as though to make sure his excellent Spanish permitted full expression of what was on his mind. He leaned earnestly toward Lindquist.

"You come here, knowing we promised you death if you returned. You sit with us and tell us the soldiers' plans. Even how you sent some of them on the wrong trail. You tell us the Utes have joined them. You make it possible for us to lay traps — even perhaps for us to drive our enemies from these canyons. Because of these things we have permitted you a seat among us. But how can you beg for the lives of soldiers when by what you have done you have already killed them?"

Lindquist reached out and indicated the knife at Juanito's belt. The chief uncertainly drew the weapon and handed it across. Lindquist cut one of the thongs with which the sleeve of his jacket was fringed, adding another gap in this trimming to those already existing there — bits of leather used over the seasons for small repairs and wrappings in a dozen situations where substitutes were unavailable. Returning the knife, he stretched the thong between his two hands. And he began to speak.

At one end were the Navajo. At the other end of the thong was the Army. The Navajo were defending their homeland — their crops and stock — their families — their lives. Perhaps, most of all, their pride. On the other hand, the Army was carrying out the orders of its biggest chiefs — not chiefs in the field like Carson, great as he was — but the orders of important, distant men whom Navajo arrows could never reach. Men safe from the bullets of the longest Navajo guns. And the Army was trained to the last man to carry out orders, even if it meant death for every soldier. These were the two forces at work, and already the thong between them was stretched to the limit of its strength.

Juanito and his Council followed Lindquist intently, nodding understanding and assent. What the leather man said was true. Soon the thong must break. When it did, there would be open war. They were prepared for this. With what he had told them of the Army's plans, they would empty their canyons of soldiers. The trouble would be done. There would no longer be the threat of the Long Walk into unfriendly country for the Navajo nation.

Lindquist shook his head stubbornly.

"A man doesn't put out a fire by throwing sticks at it," he argued. "The sticks snuff only a few sparks when they strike, then they become fuel for the flames, themselves. A small fire is put out by water. A big one is put out by setting another fire against it. And this is a big fire."

The Indian circle nodded again, respectful of the imagery Lindquist employed, for it was upon this kind of appeal that the best of their own oratory was based. But Lindquist had not yet made a major point they were willing to concede.

"You have another fire to set against the soldiers?" Juanito challenged.

Lindquist held up the thong still stretched between his two fists.

"In man hands," he said. "Let the thong break — let soldiers die, even to the last man in uniform on the mesas, and I tell you nothing has been done. There will be more soldiers, even some of the guns-on-wheels which blew up the Spanish church at Taos when it was made into a fort. Ask some of your young men who were there of that. There are more soldiers than there are Navajo. In the end those of you who are left will have to surrender or see the last of your people die. It is better to keep the thong tight — not to let it break."

Juanito studied Lindquist's hands and the taut strip of leather between them.

"It can't be done!" he growled.

Lindquist leaned sharply, earnestly forward.

"I think so," he contradicted. "The Army hunts you. Suppose the soldiers can find no Navajo. Suppose they find only empty tracks in the sand. Suppose they lose horses and supplies but the tracks they find lead nowhere. Suppose they march through Canyon de Chelly and Canyon del Muerto and meet no bullets, no arrows, nothing. How long will they stay here when they suffer nuisance but no hurt and every day proves more clearly that those they hunt could, if they wished, destroy a force twice as strong?"

"You said the soldiers would die to obey orders," the Navajo chief pointed out.

"They would. But how can they when they can find no one to kill them, none to capture — nothing at all but dust and many small troubles?" Lindquist suddenly dropped the taut thong and spread his hands expressively. "It may not work, but there's little to lose."

An elder of the Council spoke. The chief looked about the circle. His eyes swung back to Lindquist. Some of the impassiveness was gone from his face. Lindquist thought he presently might grin.

"You have a plan for this," he said slowly. "The Council will try it. . . ." He paused and picked up the strip of leather Lindquist had dropped, stretching it tight again. It snapped in his hands. He dropped the pieces. "Should that happen," he continued, "should it break because the sol-

190

diers have drawn it tighter than the Navajo, you will be the first to die!"

Lindquist nodded acceptance of this condition. The grin he had anticipated on Juanito's face materialized. A wicked, mocking thing.

"Perhaps you die soon," he added.

Lindquist scowled. The chief gestured toward the edge of the shelf. Rick twisted around. Standing between two Navajo who had obviously brought her up the cliff face as he had been brought was Micaela Castaneda. A grimed, bloodstained, distraught figure who might have been where she stood through much of the parley just finished. The deviltry in an Indian could take many shapes. Lindquist came to his feet. Juanito confronted him accusingly.

"Perhaps you only tell us what you want us to hear, after all," he said quietly. "Maybe you make clever lies. You tell us much, but nothing about the woman, about why she is here, asking like a crazy one where you are. I tell you again, it is better to die than to lie to us!"

"What do you want me to do to convince you?" Lindquist grated in sudden anger. "Cut off my head and hand it to you in a basket? Get out of my way!"

Angry as he was, he had better judgment

than to put a hand to the person of the chief. However, Juanito had wisdom also. He stepped quickly aside, and Lindquist crossed to Micaela. She broke from the two Indians beside her and flung herself against him.

"Rick!" she choked. "Rick, I — I couldn't be sure you'd be able to make them listen. I — I was afraid for you, and they had to know what they're up against. He wouldn't let me come into the canyon after you. I killed him, Rick! I killed him to find you."

"Wait a minute!" Lindquist said sharply, all too keenly aware Juanito was an interested and comprehending listener. The edge in his voice helped restore Micaela's control.

"Lieutenant Grayson, Rick. I killed him."

"You what?" The question was torn from Lindquist. "Steve?"

"Two Utes had me. They quarreled and I escaped them. Lieutenant Grayson found me. He wanted to go on and locate Captain Pfieffer. But I had to get here in case —"

"In case the Navajo killed me first and listened to what I had to say afterward? Go on."

"Lieutenant Grayson tried to keep me with him. I tricked him — got his gun. We struggled for it and fell. The gun went off. His head, Rick . . ."

"Sure he was dead?" Lindquist asked.

The girl nodded. "I can tell you where —"

Lindquist cut her short. "Not now."

"But you can't just — just leave him lying out there!"

"It won't bother him now. There's too much to be done and too little time left to worry about a dead man."

"Rick, he was your friend!"

"Friends die too. I learned that a long time ago. Did the Utes — well — treat you all right?"

The girl nodded again but started to back away as though she had discovered a facet to Eric Lindquist which either frightened her or made her sick. Lindquist could not be sure which, but he could spare no time to find out. He wondered if this accident of chance and the uniformed figure lying in the sun somewhere up on the south mesa hadn't destroyed all that he had tried to accomplish here. The same thought seemed to have appealed to Chief Juanito. He spoke quietly.

"It seems a difficult thing to keep from killing soldiers, eh, señor?"

FOURTEEN

The sound of voices seemed to come from a long distance. There was something hot in his throat. Steve Grayson choked and climbed toward the vague words he could hear.

"Lieutenant!" There was a pause.

"Hold him up a little straighter and get another shot down him. He'll come around. Nothing the matter with him but that nick in his scalp."

Grayson recognized the voice. It belonged to Captain Pfieffer. It was annoyed and crisply military. A little too much of both, under the circumstances. Grayson resented it. He resented it considerably. He opened his eyes and quit leaning against the trooper supporting him. He blinked accusingly at Captain Pfieffer.

"Nothing the matter, sir?" he said thickly and aggrievedly. "No, sir. I've just been killed is all. Shot through the head."

Pfieffer was under apparent stress. In fact, he seemed a little on the angry side.

"Get hold of yourself, Lieutenant!" he snapped. "You're barely creased and in sound enough marching condition. We heard a shot. Were you in contact with the hostiles? How many of them? What direction did they take?"

Grayson climbed unsteadily to his feet and found the effort less costly than he feared. He felt genuinely disappointed. He considered various answers to Pfieffer's questions and found none of them satisfactory. It was the curse of a military man's life that he was professionally forced to deal in fact, and fact alone. A little permissible embroidery now would save acute embarrassment. But he had no choice.

Pfieffer, who gave every indication of becoming a first-class martinet of the old school by the time he achieved his majority, listened with rising impatience. Grayson's account of events from sunrise onward had a ring of the incredulous and the impossible, even in his own ears. When he was finished, Pfieffer swore with considerable feeling if no particular skill.

"We're fighting a war out here, mister! The word is spelled W-A-R! This is a military campaign against a known enemy and with certain very clear objectives — not a furtherance of personal differences between you and Eric Lindquist or a campaign for the seduction of a Mexican wench!"

"Yes, sir," Grayson said with admirable restraint.

"You've permitted a self-admitted traitor to carry aid and comfort to the enemy. You've transmitted false information and guidance to the unit to which you were attached. You've allowed the loss of a female being held in protective custody. And you've incurred a personal casualty, reducing your physical fitness to your command."

"Yes, sir," Grayson agreed again, adding in a feeble attempt at clarification: "I got myself shot."

"It's regrettable that women are such poor marksmen!" Captain Pfieffer observed. "Return at once to headquarters with a report for Colonel Carson. I am proceeding immediately into Canyon de Chelly via the trail both Lindquist and the girl apparently used. My purpose is to locate and retake both of them. This done, I shall proceed down the canyon to a junction with Captain Carey as originally ordered."

"Yes, sir."

"I suggest the colonel employ his Ute scouts to reach the head of the canyon and make a descent from there to round up any hostile stragglers who may retreat in that direction."

"Yes, sir."

"You understand the report fully, Lieutenant?"

"Yes, sir," Grayson said stiffly. "But now that Lindquist has joined the Navajo, he may make real trouble. Maybe the colonel will want to alter the general plan."

"It's his privilege. I'm sure you can give him excellent counsel. If there is change, a courier can reach me in the canyon. On your way, Lieutenant!"

Grayson found his hat but could not pull it on over the wound above his ear. He turned away. Captain Pfieffer remounted his grinning company and they trotted briskly off toward the rim of the canyon, following the general directions toward the head of the foot trail implied in Grayson's report of events.

At the first shelter he reached, Grayson paused to watch them from sight. His head hurt and he began nursing resentment, building up a fine series of replies which could have been made to Captain Pfieffer if he had only thought them up in time. Replies which would have remained within the boundaries permissible between an inferior officer and his superior and still have really cut Pfieffer down to size. They made him feel better, as did a rather hopeful appraisal of some of the things Pfieffer's command might encounter as a result of Rick Lindquist's presence among the Navajo.

There was the Castaneda girl too. If the sample she had given him meant anything, the captain's intention to retake her might lead to considerable difficulty in itself. Grayson sincerely hoped so. The more he thought about it, the more pleased he became. He wanted to chuckle, but his head hurt too much. He struck off through the timber.

A little later, when his resentment toward Pfieffer had cooled to a reasonable level, something else occurred to him and his anger rose again. The trail Pfieffer intended to use to reach the canyon floor was a foot trail. He would have to dismount his detachment at the head of the trail and return his horses under guard to headquarters, every saddle empty. But he had seen fit to dispatch a critically wounded man across the mesa with a message for the colonel — afoot! This was, Grayson decided, what was meant when there were discussions of the brutality of modern warfare.

It was after two in the afternoon when Grayson emerged from a timber stand and approached a sentry lazing at an outpost of the headquarters camp. Maybe it was after three. Grayson didn't care. He'd come a long way. If he'd taken his time, it was because he was a casualty, wounded and dismounted. If delivery of the message entrusted to him had been delayed — perhaps even enough for Captain Pfieffer to have worked himself into a thoroughly nasty spot — he had an ironclad consolation. He had traveled as swiftly and directly as a wounded man could be expected to manage.

The sentry took a square look at him as he approached and shouted for the sergeant of the guard a good deal louder than was necessary. Grayson had hoped to attract as little attention as possible on arrival at camp. Afoot, suffering, draining his last strength, so to speak, to bring a dispatch through, he would have liked to make something of his entry. He would have attempted to do so except for knowing Pfieffer and some of those with him would be at great pains to tell a widely different story of his brush with death when the whole command was again reunited.

Avoiding curious troopers, he got to Colonel Carson's tent as rapidly as possible. The colonel dismissed the lingering sergeant who had escorted him in with a promptness which betrayed a sympathy and compassion not warped by lifelong devotion to military codes.

"What in hell happened to you, son?" Carson asked with real interest when the sergeant was gone.

Grayson was severely tempted. He could have made his report a harrowing one of personal misfortune, hardship, and devotion to duty. But the honor of an officer and a gentleman sustained him. With the exception of occasional inadvertent lapses into profanity when his powers of expression fell short of the demands upon them — lapses which seemed to amuse the colonel vastly — he delivered an amazingly straightforward military brief of the day, concluding dutifully with Pfieffer's message.

Carson studied the tips of his fingers. He polished the toe caps of both boots on the back of the opposite leg. He stood up and took a turn about the tent. Finally he opened a case and rummaged somewhat untidily in his gear until he found a stone flagon. He brought this back to his field table, hammered the dust from a pair of service cups, and filled both of them. He pushed one to Grayson.

"Your health, Lieutenant," he proposed.

"You look like you need it."

Grayson lifted the cup. It contained a muddy brown volatile fluid. The whiskey took hold before it reached his lips, powerful fumes stinging his nostrils. And what he swallowed was liquid fire. He looked at the colonel with rounded eyes. Carson was swallowing with evident relish.

A spasm shook Grayson, but he emptied the cup. After a long moment he was able to get his breath. It came with a long rushing sound the colonel mistook for a sigh of satisfaction.

"The Army's sending better men out here every season," Carson said in open approval. He indicated Grayson's cup. "That's Taos Lightnin'. Fellow up above there at Rio Hondo's got some corn and a still. He makes it. Always uses stone jugs. He says glass bottles get eaten away too fast. Might be, at that. But it's the best whiskey west of the Missouri. Everybody says so. And they don't get any argument. It's the *only* whiskey west of the Missouri. It takes a real man to drink it."

"Yes, sir," Grayson agreed earnestly, and he quickly put his hand over his cup as Carson lifted the flagon to refill it.

The colonel drank slowly. He put his cup down and studied Grayson, a blandly prying scrutiny with no evidence of satisfaction or disapproval. He said nothing for several moments. Grayson, like most junior officers in the command, had accepted Carson's authority on this expedition as the wisest choice of command possible with little further thought. New Mexico was Carson's country. He was a sort of magician at reducing hostiles to subjection. He had already bought his place in history.

For the first time Grayson now had his doubts about the man. Certainly Carson was not playing the part of a commander caught in the field with an inferior force against an overpowering and elusive enemy. He was taking things mighty easy for a CO with detachments now afield in an effort to contact the foe and engage him.

"What do you make of old Rick Lindquist?" Carson asked suddenly.

It was a man-to-man question, rank aside for the moment. Grayson felt the sort of paternal camaraderie of his reception in Carson's headquarters definitely called for a man-to-man answer. He uncovered his whiskey cup and let the colonel fill it again, after all. He took a deep, burning swallow and taxed his vocabulary to the limit. He spoke in full detail and with naked honesty concerning Eric Lindquist.

Carson nodded thoughtfully. "I suppose so," he agreed. "There's sure been times when I've added him up about that way myself. There was once at Bent's fort. He waited till the last minute, then showed up with a bale of beaver plew that won the post jackpot for top price per pelt at a bare ten per cent a skin better than the showing I made. And me figuring I had the pot sewed up all along."

Carson paused and chuckled a little.

"He turned around then and gambled my catch off of me at faro and wound up trading me a spavined Arapaho cayuse for the best little old mountain pony I ever owned. But there's something about him. Rick's toes are most always pointed at something when he makes tracks."

"Purgatory!" Grayson said with deep feeling.

"Hunh?"

"Hell!" Grayson explained. "I hope his toes are pointed for hell this time!"

"He'll have company," Carson said with a grin. "I reckon most of us out here are headed that way for one reason or another, son. Leastways, that's the way they tell it back on the River."

He paused and frowned. "Trouble with

Rick is, he'll take his own good time getting there. Matter of fact, he's so stubborn he just might prove folks back on the River are wrong. Rick's got a conscience. Ever notice that?"

"No!"

"Well, he has, just the same. Not everybody can afford one. 'Specially out here. I never knew a man who could handle Indians better than Rick. We'd be in a tight spot in these mesas without him."

Grayson was shocked. It seemed impossible Kit Carson could so shallowly estimate a man's villainy.

"With your permission, sir," he said, "we're in a bad spot here *because* of him!"

Carson put a hand kindly to Grayson's knee.

"You're kind of winded, son. You've had a hard day. Better get one of the boys to dress that nick in your scalp. Then turn in and get some rest."

Grayson stood up and found the crossbar of the tent poles squarely in front of his nose. He ducked under this and straightened again as crisply as he could manage.

"I request permission, sir, to clean up and report back in half an hour for assignment to duty. The situation being what it is, every available man in the command should be in the field."

Carson lifted the flagon, looked at it again, and corked it with obvious regret. He glanced up at Grayson.

"Son, save your breath and quit breathing so hard. You're fighting Indians now. Surest way to get yourself whipped is to get in too big a hurry. You've already reported to me for today. If you've got to do it again, make it in a couple of hours and report to Señor Castaneda. He may want to know what you can tell him about his daughter. I'm going to take a nap."

Grayson saluted and backed from the tent. Outside he paused to look back, wondering if Pfieffer was such a martinet, after all. At least Pfieffer was a soldier. And soldiers didn't nap on campaign.

Moving toward the bivouacs of the camp, Grayson gave considerable care to his choice of a man to dress his wound. He picked a mild, closemouthed young trooper who had shown marked knowledge and medical skill. With the blood washed away, the trooper's examination was brief, almost careless.

"Bullet no more than just touched you, Lieutenant."

"The skull — the skull's not injured?"

"Scalp's split a mite is all. You could have got worse hurt stubbing your toe."

On the basis of this diagnosis, Grayson felt obliged to waive bandaging. He tidied up his tunic as best he could and moved on down the line to the shelter he had surrendered to Pablo Castaneda and his daughter. The old man was dozing. He roused at Grayson's entry. He seemed in no way distraught. Grayson wondered if Pablo Castaneda had been advised of the serious risk involved in his daughter's disappearance. And because of this uncertainty he launched his account carefully and with some nicety of feeling.

Castaneda listened quietly, and it became apparent to Grayson that Micaela's father had no misconception of the dangers facing his daughter. However, he showed no real excitement until Grayson revealed that Micaela had escaped from the Utes who had captured her. He nodded delightedly. Grayson thought the delight ill became the old man.

"She said — she said she killed them," he repeated, returning to the Utes.

"But of course!" Castaneda agreed. "How else could she escape them?"

"A girl just doesn't kill a couple of Indians like that!" Grayson protested.

The old man shrugged. "It is the country, señor," he said. "You do not understand it yet. The things one learns to do here to live. Micaela had learned well. Always she has been quick to learn. The Navajo who were our friends are good teachers. They hate the Utes. You are fortunate, señor, that she did not kill you as well. She is quite clever with a gun."

Grayson felt his temper slipping. "That was an accident!"

Micaela's father smiled. "One learns to cling to life by such accidents on these mesas, Lieutenant."

Grayson felt obliged to retreat. It seemed unlikely he would be able to impress Castaneda with the danger yet facing Micaela among the Navajo and in the company of a thorough reprobate like Eric Lindquist. It was his opinion senility had set in with a vengeance on the old man, possibly as a result of the loss of his *estancia*. Otherwise there was no accounting for so unnatural a father.

Moving down through the camp, he found an empty tent and flopped down. Rolling his jacket beneath his aching head for additional pillow, he tried to rationalize the situation in this so-called headquarters camp.

Micaela and Lindquist were among the Navajo. If they had both survived their forbidden return to de Chelly, one or both was now plotting with the Indians to upset the whole campaign of the military. Captain Pfieffer had altered his objectives and was now en route to the canyon floor, intending to engage the hostile immediately and certain to contact them since he was entering their stronghold. Carey's force was at the mouth of the canyon or near it, a considerable distance away, and completely separated from this impending initial engagement. The position of all forces was by now known to the enemy. If a military situation ever desperately required clarification and realignment, this was it. Yet the colonel commanding was napping in his tent!

Grayson fell to wondering earnestly about Kit Carson as he had earlier wondered about Rick Lindquist, combing the man's personality for a single thread he might understand and follow. He realized the Army departmental command operated on the theory of using the best weapons available in employing men like Lindquist and Carson for penetration of given areas. But it was a theory which had grave faults.

If a man was going to be practical about it — which he must be when the lives of himself and his comrades were at stake — if he was going to wipe away all the tall stuff of legends — these hunters and trappers and so-called scouts were misfits wherever they were used. There was something wrong in their past life or in their thinking which made them head for that fringe of decent living known as the frontier. There was something wrong in them which made them remain at these outposts of civilization, shunning continually their fellow men and seeking always the lonely places.

Lindquist had already demonstrated he was a thorough renegade, quitting the command to which he was attached and going over to the Indians. And not even with apology or guilt. Instead, the man had actually been driven by a personal determination to betray which left him no time even to go to the aid of a white woman in the hands of the admittedly unpredictable Utes. He guessed it was this, most of all, that he couldn't figure in Lindquist, rather than merely his desertion to the Navajo. When two forces were opposed, a decent man might have valid reasons for siding with one or the other. But nothing that called itself a man could have reason for abandoning a woman of his own kind when she was in desperate danger.

Carson was somewhat a different matter. His integrity was beyond question. He was a great man. To be around him was to feel it. And a civilian — regardless of temporary rank — was not given command of a force such as Carson had enjoyed repeatedly except under conditions of implicit trust and the immense superiority of the chosen man for a particular assignment over the most highly trained military personnel.

Nevertheless, Carson also seemed subject to prior loyalties. Certainly he showed no evidence of Grayson's own bitterness over Lindquist's defection. He had waived Grayson's mischances with Lindquist and Micaela without a trace of Captain Pfieffer's explosive asperity. And although it must be as apparent to him as it was to Grayson himself that Pfieffer was courting entrapment and destruction by entering de Chelly via the foot trail, he had shown no alarm and no inclination to provide Pfieffer with either support or diversion. He had, in fact, ignored the captain's request for a Ute sally to the head of the main canyon to intercept stragglers.

Fighting off drowsiness in the midafternoon heat of the tent, Steve Grayson came to the reluctant conclusion that, whatever his personal reasons might be, Colonel Carson was in his way as unwilling as Lindquist had been to see launched a full-scale military attack which might drive the Navajo from their canyons. With this uncomfortable belief for a bedfellow, Grayson finally dropped off into the sleep he badly needed.

FIFTEEN

For more than an hour after Micaela's arrival on the ledge where the Navajo Council had set up headquarters, Lindquist was busy with Chief Juanito and the old men. There was much to be done. The Navajo had prepared the defense of the canyons according to a habit which was the result of generations of practice. Their forces had been widely scattered to cover all possible points of attack. The strength at each point was based wholly upon the ease of its defense and the apparent likelihood of attack. As a consequence, an invading force had only to divide itself into a couple of diversionary groups commissioned to launch false sallies and then hit with its main force at the most easily defended and least likely to approach point in the Navajo perimeter. This guaranteed the weakest Navajo party to face.

Lindquist first dictated a new dispersal to Juanito, so that the Navajo were broken into small, flexible groups without fixed points to defend but under orders to remain hidden and hold themselves ready to move swiftly into any threatened area. Organizing a defense was complicated by Lindquist's uncertainty over Carson's over-all strategy.

There seemed no basic reason for delaying full-scale movement against the Navajo, since this was the admitted purpose of the campaign. Yet Carson was certainly in no hurry about this. And instead of reserving his main force, keeping it available at headquarters, Carson had curiously divided his whole command into two parties under Carey and Pfieffer, and then further aggravated this division by sending his two captains to opposite ends of the canyon system, separating them by a good thirty miles.

The man's record for generalship made doubting his wisdom in this deployment impossible, and it was uncomfortable to know Kit Carson was in command of opposing forces without also having the advantage of some inkling of his real intentions. Certainly the chief of scouts was preparing to draw some kind of trick out of his possibles bag after these first misleading movements. Rick Lindquist would have gladly traded another night's sleep, hand running, to know what that trick was.

When the couriers had been all sent out,

the sentries posted, and reports of all Navajo positions confirmed, Juanito descended into the canyon to take active command of the one mounted party Lindquist thought it advisable to keep on hand. The canyon system moved them into an inevitable period of waiting, shot with the concern of any gambling man that he held the right cards for the coming play.

For the first time now with a moment of his own, Lindquist looked for Micaela and a chance to talk with her. He found her in a cranny in the ledge under a borrowed blanket splendid enough in pattern and weave to have belonged to Chief Juanito himself. She was sleeping heavily. Lindquist eased against the wall near her, settling himself without waking her, and let his body sleep while his mind worked, as a man will when his problems are greater than his weariness.

In spite of the fact he had been busy, Lindquist was troubled by the realization Micaela had made no further attempt to approach him. He had a feeling she had actually avoided him since his refusal to make a sortie onto the south mesa to recover Steve Grayson's body. It was hard to make many men understand where to draw a practical line between brutal callousness

and unalterable fact. It was even more difficult to convince a woman, with her more
cloying devotion to at least the outward evi-
dences of affection and decency. Yet it was
a lesson learned early in the mountains.
Too often the survival of the living de-
pended upon abandonment of the dead.

The horse tribes of the plains, fanatical
in their attempts to rescue their dead from
the field of battle and so prevent mutila-
tion of the bodies by the enemy, still occasionally retreated and left fallen comrades
behind. And an Indian did not have the
white conviction that a man did not live in
his body after death. Burials among most
of the tribes included food and comforts
for a journey, and there was a widespread
belief that the spirit of a body abandoned
or mutilated died as the body died.

Lindquist wondered if the girl's concern
over Steve Grayson stemmed from something like this, something pagan absorbed
from the Navajo. He shrugged the thought
off as improbable. Her Spanish ancestry
would insure spiritual strength, proof
against any paganism. Her concern, therefore, had to be on a basis of personal loss,
perhaps in part upon her guilt in the accident which had cost Grayson his life. At
least what she had called an accident.

215

It seemed wise to be brutally practical in considering this also. Remembering the lip-licking Grayson had gone through when he first saw the girl, Lindquist suspected the struggle between them had been over something a little more specific than the direction either was to travel. Without the prospect of some pleasantry to absorb Grayson's attention and to stir instinctive defense in Micaela, it seemed incredible Grayson would have permitted himself to be disarmed or that the girl would have shot him, either by accident or intent.

On the basis of this reasoning, Grayson should have died and his body left to rot in the sun. For many small services and a lifetime of devotion, for smallness of body and staggering handicaps in a world based on physical strength, Lindquist believed a woman's right was freedom from the persuasion of strength. A man who denied her this right was the ultimate coward.

Yet none of this satisfactorily explained Micaela's deep distress over Grayson's death and Lindquist's own subsequent refusal to attempt recovery of the body. Micaela had seen two Utes die earlier in the day. She had admittedly killed one of them herself. The act of causing death could not therefore distress her greatly.

There remained only the conclusion that she had not wanted Grayson to die, whatever the circumstances or justification. And in death she wanted the vague consolation of service paid the body. So it boiled down like a stew to the meat of the matter, regardless of how agilely Lindquist looked for another explanation. She had wanted Grayson, loved him.

This was distasteful thinking. Lindquist accepted it because he could not do otherwise. He turned his mind away from the girl before he began measuring his own attitude toward her. But he could not dispose of Grayson so readily. The young lieutenant, for all his stiff-necked military stuffiness on occasion, had been a first-class saddle companion. A man met all too few such in a lifetime. As soldiers went, Grayson had been one of the best, in spite of his inexperience.

In a way a man's life was a series of losses, since he had to face repeatedly the death of friends. He grew accustomed to this, even resigned to it, but there was always regret. Lindquist had considered Steve Grayson a friend. His regret was sincere.

Long shadows were beginning to darken the ledge when Lindquist awoke with a start. It was perhaps four o'clock, and the sun was still high on the mesas, but within the towering walls of de Chelly it was already early evening. Straightening, twisting the cramp from his shoulders and back, where they had been leaning against the wall, he saw Micaela was awake under her blanket and looking steadily at him.

For a moment he thought awareness of her look or something she had said had roused him. Then he became aware of a stir at the parapet on the outer edge of the shelf. A man climbing the trail below this hailed again, and he knew this was what had broken his sleep. A moment later the man climbed over the parapet, excitedly calling a message. Lindquist rose stiffly and crossed as the members of the Council gathered about the messenger. The man started delivery of a swift report in Navajo. Lindquist turned and signaled imperatively to Micaela. She crawled unhurriedly from her blanket and approached.

Lindquist indicated the messenger. Micaela listened to the swift sing of Navajo syllables for several moments. Lindquist, watching her impatiently, thought she was making every effort to prevent what she heard from showing on her face. He was irritated. Finally she turned to him.

"Soldiers on the foot trail across the canyon," she translated. "The sentry stationed at the top came down ahead of them. He says they rode right up to the top of the trail as though they knew exactly how to find it They ate, left their horses with six men as guards, and started down the trail. Chief Juanito wants to know what is to be done."

"Captain Pfieffer?" Lindquist asked sharply. "Is that who it is? Is it Captain Pfieffer's party?"

Micaela shrugged and indicated the breathless courier. "How could he know?"

Lindquist gripped her arm. "I'm asking you. You were up there earlier."

"I didn't see Captain Pfieffer. I only saw Lieutenant Grayson."

"Listen," Lindquist growled. "Be a little help, can't you? This is important!"

"Did I get help when I got here this afternoon and asked for it?" Micaela asked. "You're a big man, Rick Lindquist. Big and hard — and empty inside. You don't need help. Don't ask for it. I'm just interpreting for you."

"That's for sure!" Lindquist snapped. "So it's still Grayson! What could I have done for him? I couldn't bring him back to life for you. I came over to try to make you understand, but you were asleep."

"There are some things I can't understand," Micaela said firmly.

"It looks like. All right. But if these Navajo mean anything to you, I need more than interpreting now. You say the soldiers rode directly to the head of the trail?"

Micaela pointed to the courier. "I didn't say it. He did."

Lindquist struggled with his impatience. It vanished abruptly before a sudden thought. He caught the girl's arm.

"All right," he said quietly, the conviction forming in his mind giving him, to his surprise, as much pleasure as he knew it would give her. "So you're being stubborn and nasty. Maybe you'll force me into doing something about Steve Grayson after all. Maybe I'll have to bring him back to life for you."

Micaela paled. "Do you have to make a joke of that?"

"I'm not joking. Listen, how did those soldiers find the head of that trail across the canyon so easily? They have to be Pfieffer's detachment. Somebody had to guide them to the head of that trail. The Navajo certainly didn't do it. You know where it is. I found it. So did two Utes. And so did Steve Grayson. You and I are down here. The two Utes are dead. Who does that leave? Grayson is alive — alive enough to have led or directed Pfieffer's party to the head of the trail!"

Micaela stared at him for a long moment. Suddenly she wavered a little and tilted against him, her head against the dusty black-stained leather of his jacket.

"Rick!" she breathed. "It's true! It has to be! It must be!"

Her hair was beneath his chin. He touched it gently and was immediately embarrassed by the clumsiness of the gesture.

"We'll find out," he promised.

She straightened and turned to the waiting courier with swift, terse questions. The courier answered in detail.

"That's about all he can tell us," Micaela reported. "Forty soldiers — maybe more — working their way down from South Mesa — very slowly." She paused and smiled. "It takes a long time to learn how to climb down the steps of the ancients with any speed."

Lindquist nodded. "I know. Send this man back to Juanito. Tell the chief to take his horsemen down the canyon to the big trail. Tell him to keep out of sight from above and move quietly. He's to take the big trail to the mesa top and detour wide around Carson's camp. He'll have plenty of time, I think. Tell him to capture the horses Pfieffer left at the head of the foot trail. We don't want the guards killed. No dead horses. He'll have to watch that. But get the horses. Bring them back into the canyon and hide them."

Micaela repeated the message in Navajo to the courier. The man started to leave. Lindquist checked him.

"I'll need the Navajo foot party stationed down in the canyon at the Monuments. Have them keep out of sight, too, but move up to the bottom of the foot trail. I'll meet them there."

This order was also passed. The elders of the Council listened soberly, appraising Lindquist's moves. One or two grinned a little as Micaela translated, and one made a joke which brought a soft run of laughter. Lindquist thought Micaela colored at this, but the courier repeated an instruction of which he was not sure and she clarified it for him, so that Lindquist had no chance to ask her what brought the laughter among the Council.

The courier stepped back over the edge of the parapet and climbed down toward the floor of the canyon. Lindquist started to follow him. Micaela stepped past him and reached a small foot into the first of the toe holds staggered dizzyingly downward into space. When Lindquist started to protest, she smiled back up at him.

"I changed the message you sent out a little, Rick," she said blandly. "The message to the Navajo footmen at the Monuments was to meet *us* at the bottom of the foot trail. I forgot you couldn't understand old Kubichi's joke when he heard me do this."

"I wondered about the laugh."

"I'll tell you about it," Micaela promised. But she did not. Releasing her hold on the edge of the parapet, she started swiftly down the cliff after the courier. Lindquist swung his own leg over the edge and stepped into the first of the toe holds.

Reaching the canyon floor, Lindquist and Micaela detoured down the canyon along the base of the north wall until a bend hid any chance of their crossing being spotted by Pfieffer's soldiers on the opposite cliff. They dodged across to the south wall and worked back up toward the bottom of the foot trail down from South Mesa.

When they arrived at this, the Navajo party from the Monuments had already appeared. Micaela's insistence on accompanying him seemed less of a nuisance to Lindquist then. It proved far more effective to issue orders through her directly into Navajo than to rely on the comprehension of the few Indians in the party who might understand Spanish.

Warning them they faced certain risks, he picked the four whom the others of the party nominated as the best bowmen. The rest he stationed among covering rocks to check recklessness on Pfieffer's part should his main ruse fail — their orders to use their guns only as a last resort. Keeping the bowmen with him, he sat down to wait. And remembering his own deliberation in the descent of the trail reaching upward from their position, he waited in patience. Micaela scooped a small depression into the warm sand beside the rock on which he sat and curled up like a kitten in this. Presently the stone under him became hard and Lindquist was uncomfortable, but he wouldn't join the girl on the sand. He knew he should have chosen the sand for its greater comfort in the first place and he was reluctant to admit his error.

It was small-boy business, this refusal to change his position, and he knew it. Something to do with the girl. He knew this also.

But he remained uncomfortably on the rock, stiff-backed until humor at his own folly forced him to move down beside Micaela. When he was settled there he continued to grin. In some ways he was as stiff-backed as Steve Grayson — at least where this girl was concerned. If she was aware of his stubbornness or his self-amusement, she said nothing.

Far above there was sound. The faint click of metal against stone. An imprecation was jolted from a startled and alarmed trooper when his foot slipped without warning from some uncertain purchase. Lindquist chuckled again. He thought the descending troopers would be about in the right state of mind when they reached the last stage of the descent to insure the success of the plan he had in mind.

Micaela glanced at him again with this second chuckle, but still she said nothing. They continued to wait. She closed her eyes and dozed a little. The Navajo bowmen were motionless, shadows as inert and impersonal as the rocks among which they stood. Lindquist studied Micaela with considerably more frankness than he could have contrived were her eyes or the eyes of others upon them.

He thought of the thousand times he

had sat like this, waiting. Waiting on a hunt. Sometimes for meat or profit. Sometimes for an enemy. Quiet, lonely waits in quiet, lonely places. Usually alone. Occasionally with another of his kind. Part of a wild way of life with nothing in it but solitude and the freedom of being alone, of owing no obligation but to himself, of pinning his life recklessly to the sights of his rifle and his woodcraft and his stubbornness. The life he wanted. The life which satisfied him.

Yet waiting like this was better. There was something here which was better than anything he had ever known. Something he wanted with a peculiar insistence which troubled him. Something which had made him side with the Navajo when he knew they had no real chance against the penalties assessed against them. Something more than his conviction there was no justice in the thing Carson had been ordered to accomplish in Canyon de Chelly.

The girl beside him was a part of that want. How much a part he wasn't sure. But it went beyond her — far beyond. He was glad of this. It left him something when she was gone. And she would be gone sooner or later. It was painfully apparent that Steve Grayson had put the first mark on Micaela. And as he had told her, Grayson must certainly be alive.

To have merely something left of what he wanted here did not satisfy Rick Lindquist. Still, it could be made to do. A man was seldom satisfied completely. And at least there remained something for which he was willing to fight.

A nut-sized stone bounded out into space, somewhere above. It was hissing with the speed of its fall when it struck a few yards from Lindquist. He shifted and looked up. Two troopers had emerged from a crevice which formed a portion of the lower part of the trail. They stood at the brink of the last smooth pitch of stone, eying the worn steps traversing it. Silhouetted against the night sky, so much lighter than the deep shadows of de Chelly, they were clearly visible. Lindquist nodded to his bowmen.

A Navajo raised and bent his weapon. Starshine winked on the silver with which the heavy leather bow guard on his left wrist was decorated. The bowstring sang. An arrow streaked wickedly upward to strike fire from the stone directly between the two troopers. It was superlative shooting, carrying out Lindquist's orders to shoot close but not into flesh as closely as could be done. The troopers stared for a moment in startled surprise, each measuring how close death had been to him. As though on strings, they leaped back from sight with awkward haste.

A hail started at their position and traveled back up the canyon wall, following the trail as it was passed from man to man along it. That it traveled in this fashion indicated the officer in command of the detachment was with the rear guard near the summit, rather than at the head of his men. Lindquist was a little disappointed. He did not like Pfieffer and had hoped to deal directly with him rather than with one of his men.

The hail was answered at the top by an order which was passed back down the trail, man to man, at a much lower level of voice. Lindquist saw two heads, widely separated at the top of the pitch above him, poke cautiously into view. A pair of the Navajo bowmen stepped into the open, accepting the risk Lindquist had promised them. They loosed a pair of arrows, and the heads ducked from sight. Gunfire rattled higher up. Lead sang at the bowmen. But vertical shooting was apt to be inaccurate and the bowmen leaped back to shelter, unharmed. Lindquist drew a deep breath of relief and satisfaction and grinned at Micaela.

"Now we'll see what kind of medicine we can make," he said. And he lifted his voice in a rolling shout. "This is Lindquist. Do you hear me?"

There was a long moment of silence. Then a voice Lindquist recognized as belonging to a barrel-chested sergeant in Pfieffer's command answered him.

"You damned turncoat!"

There was another pause, during which a query was relayed down from above. The sergeant voiced it when it reached him.

"What's the idea, Lindquist?"

"The trail's closed," Lindquist shouted. "Sort of a hint for you to turn around and climb back up on the mesa, where you belong."

"Hell!" the sergeant said with feeling, not waiting for an answer to percolate down from above. "Before we'd climb this cliff again we'll eat every arrow you can throw at us!"

"You don't have to do that," Lindquist offered. "Just come on down, one man at a time. And throw your guns ahead of you. You'll like it down here. There's plenty of flat ground to stand on."

"Hope there's plenty of room to bury

you!" the man above bellowed. "We're keeping our guns!"

"Suit yourself," Lindquist agreed amiably. "We're waiting and we've got plenty of time. It's nice and comfortable here. Hope you're comfortable too."

There was a long silence. Lindquist began to enjoy the fact that the officer commanding this detachment was at the wrong end of the descent. It wasn't hard to imagine the military man's helplessness at having a thousand feet of virtually vertical single-file trail between himself and his point of contact with his enemy.

After several minutes there was a brief rattle of gunfire somewhere near the rim, followed by thin, ragged shouting. An object hissed down from above and embedded itself in the sand a dozen yards out from the base of the canyon wall. A Navajo sprinted out to retrieve it, drew only one wide shot for showing himself, and scuttled back to Lindquist. The object was a Navajo arrow. Lindquist gleefully showed it to Micaela.

"Juanito?" she asked.

He nodded. "He's closed the head of the trail now. And he's got the horses. That's what those shots and that shouting was — the top men in Pfieffer's bunch trying to cover their line of retreat against attack. Pfieffer's really boxed now. And some cavalry men we know are going to have to *walk* back to their colonel's camp."

Micaela amusedly drew a pattern in the sand.

"Señor Carson will not be happy with them for that."

"Happy!" Lindquist snorted. "He'll be fit to be tied. He'll be so mad he'll peel their hides off, salt 'em, and serve 'em fried to every man for breakfast!"

"Maybe they won't be back for breakfast."

"They'll make it, all right. Juanito will be withdrawing with the horses now. Soon as Pfieffer discovers the head of the trail isn't blocked on him any more, he'll order a retreat. He'll about have to. His men can't hang onto those rocks forever. It'll take them most of the night to climb back to the top and cross the mesa to their camp, but they'll about make it."

"You won't let them climb down here," Micaela said. She was driving at something.

"Not unless they throw their guns down first," Lindquist agreed.

Micaela nodded, her eyes dancing. "That's what I mean, Rick. You *yanquis* make good enough plans, but a Navajo understands a little of making a war too. Maybe Juanito won't let them climb back up onto the mesa as long as they have their guns, either."

"He'll have to, sooner or later."

"Of course. But will the sooner be soon enough for the soldiers? Would you like to spend all night hanging onto the rock up there? If Juanito waits a little, I think the soldiers will get very tired."

Lindquist grunted. "Juanito doubles his risk every minute he stays on the mesa now. He runs a chance Carson will send a scout out to contact Pfieffer or that one of the Utes will stumble on the situation up there and report it."

"Is that so dangerous? Colonel Carson has only a few men in his camp now. And he can't leave the camp completely unguarded. This is Captain Pfieffer's command. Who could drive Juanito away from the top of the trail but the soldiers under Captain Carey? And they are at the mouth of the canyon, thirty miles away."

For a moment Lindquist mentally kicked his backside for making a tactical error in not ordering Juanito to do just the thing Micaela was now suggesting the chief might be attempting. Then he saw the flaw in it, the real danger.

"You're forgetting Carson's Utes. I don't know how many of them there are, but more than enough to outnumber Juanito and those with him. It's no good. Besides, Juanito has his orders. I told him to pick up Pfieffer's horses and get back into the canyon with them as fast as he could!"

"I know, Rick," Micaela agreed softly. "But you forget something too. You are not the chief of the Navajo!"

Lindquist subsided under the bluntness of this reminder. There was little activity on the face of the cliff. Twice the sharp-eyed Navajo bowmen fired arrows upward in warning at impatient or unwary troopers who showed themselves, again shooting so accurately for near misses that the cavalry-men must have felt luck alone saved them in each instance.

Perhaps an hour after the last flight of arrows, distant gunfire broke out again on the rim. It continued in ragged pattern for several minutes, and the location of the sound revealed it did not involve any of Pfieffer's command pinned to the face of the cliff.

Lindquist scooped up one handful of dry sand after another, listening to the gunfire above and letting the sand run through his fingers. He believed he knew what was happening, but there was nothing he could do. His whole strategy had been based on avoidance of actual conflict between the Navajo and any element of Carson's forces. Now that was past. What he had hoped he might be able to do was undone. There was no longer any chance for the Navajo. Even the humor of Pfieffer's entrapped position evaporated. Micaela sensed his change in mood.

"The Utes?" she asked sharply.

This time Lindquist nodded. "Pretty near has to be. Like you pointed out, Carson has nobody else to move up so quickly behind Juanito. Why didn't that fool Indian get out of there and back into the canyon with those horses while he could?"

"Maybe he is winning the battle, Rick."

"I've told you it can't be done that way! Now he's drawn blood, Carson will never quit until the Navajo are cleaned out of these canyons."

"Utes are Indians, not soldiers, Rick. Maybe to kill them is different."

"They're soldiers when they're on the government pay roll," Lindquist said grimly. "Carson has to account for them the same as he does for every trooper on his rolls. The shooting has started. It can end only in two ways."

"How?"

"Complete surrender of Juanito and his people or a canyon full of dead Navajo. And the Army of the United States doesn't care which!"

SIXTEEN

Toward midnight Micaela fell asleep, her head resting against Lindquist's thigh. He sat leaning against a boulder and listening to the silence of the great canyon. There was nothing to betray the presence of the Navajo on alert guard at the foot of the trail a few yards away. And the stubborn, stranded cavalrymen pinned to the narrow track ascending the canyon wall were equally as quiet. The rim, halfway to the stars, was also silent. There was no way to know what had happened to Juanito and his mounted party.

Lindquist went carefully over the situation in his mind, detail by detail, hunting again for some maneuver by which the Navajo could be put into a position from which they could trade with Carson — some sort of compromise short of abandonment of de Chelly or annihilation. Unable to find any, he dozed, confident of the wariness of the Navajo sentries.

He was awakened a little later, jolted to instant awareness by a startled cry from one of the Indians. And at the same time an incredible rain began from above. He was a moment in identifying it. Micaela sat up, frightened by the clatter of falling objects bounding and rebounding from the canyon wall as they fell.

"Rick! Rick, what is it?"

Lindquist shook his head in utter disbelief and relief and began to laugh.

"The equipment of about forty cavalrymen," he said. "Everything but their clothes. Juanito must still have the head of the trail closed. Otherwise Captain Pfieffer would have tried to withdraw rather than this. It looks like we've outwaited the Army — persuaded Pfieffer it's smarter to drop his guns and save his men than to have them start dropping off of that rock in exhaustion."

Micaela laughed also. "Now wait till they go back to Colonel Carson — without even their guns!"

The hail of gear from above continued for a surprisingly long time. When it stopped, Lindquist's Navajo slid out onto the sand to start making recovery. The sergeant who had first hailed the canyon floor sang out in the darkness somewhere above the last pitch.

"You still there, Lindquist?" Then, not waiting for an answer, "This is going to cost you your hide! You and ever' damned one of them Indians!"

Lindquist made no answer. This was victory, but it was temporary. He was afraid the sergeant was speaking the blunt truth. Nevertheless, there was something wonderful in the audacity of the coup which had been counted on Pfieffer's force with the expenditure of but a few arrows. Its inevitable result could not for the moment detract from it.

The Navajo kept piling up arms and ammunition bandoleers until it seemed impossible forty men could have carried so much armament and weight. Sounds from above indicated the unburdened soldiery was beginning to work its way back up the cliff, making a painful withdrawal in the darkness. Lindquist checked a few of the weapons in the heap the Navajo had collected. A number had been destroyed or damaged beyond salvage in striking rock on the way down, but those which had fallen free had been safely caught by the soft sand of the canyon floor and needed only cleaning to be serviceable.

In a country and among a people where arms were as hard to come by as they were among the Navajo, this addition to the tribal arsenal was an event of major importance. Lindquist shared the elation of the

Indians for a moment until he remembered once again that this reinforcement meant at best only that a few of them would be able to postpone extinction slightly.

He gave orders for the weapons to be carried across the canyon and hidden near the ledge serving temporarily as Council headquarters. He waited where he was with Micaela for Juanito's return from the rim with Pfieffer's horses.

When the tribesmen carried away the last of the guns and silence returned, he found Micaela studying him soberly.

"You think there's absolutely no hope of holding the canyon?"

"After this? I'm sure of it!"

"How can you be?"

"Look at the facts — all of them," Lindquist said. "One fact is that the Navajo *could* accept Carson's terms for surrender. They could load up what belongings they can carry and march under guard to Bosque Redondo. A Long Walk, all right. What — about two hundred miles? Hard on the old and the kids. But they could do it. They could settle on the reservation the government has plotted out there. They wouldn't be as comfortable or as secure as they have been in de Chelly. Returns from the land wouldn't be so good. Some of them would be hungrier than they are here. But the tribe has moved before. They haven't been in de Chelly forever. They could move again."

Micaela was listening, but Lindquist realized she didn't understand the point he was trying to make.

"Couldn't they?" he prodded.

"Yes — yes, I suppose they could."

"Then why don't they?"

Micaela looked up at the strip of night sky, a narrow strip from where they sat, separating the looming walls of the canyon. She shrugged with a bitter helplessness.

"A lot of reasons, I suppose," she answered. "I am not Navajo. I know them — maybe I understand their thinking. But you're talking about facts, Rick. On that basis, I suppose what holds them here more than anything else is something a *yanqui* might not believe in — the spirits of the canyon."

"Spirits?"

"The ancients, first. A whole race. Who knows how long they lived here, how many of them there were? And after them, the Navajo. Could you guess how many Navajo have died and are buried in this canyon? Juanito's people can't give it up

240

under the eyes of that unseen audience."

"It's pride, then."

"Yes, I think so."

"I understand, all right." Lindquist nodded. "But that's the way it is with Carson's soldiers too. Pride. From the greenest trooper all the way to the old men in Washington. Pride in their service. That's what I was trying to get around when I argued that Juanito should create a nuisance rather than dive into outright fighting. Now he's fired on the Army — at least on the Utes Carson imported. There'll be no stopping the uniforms until their orders have been carried out to the last letter."

"It's wrong, Rick. It's terribly wrong!"

"I don't particularly like the Army. I've been out here long enough to know it's made almost as many mistakes as the Indians. But I will say this — a *yanqui* soldier always finishes his job. He always has. He always will — including this one."

"Colonel Carson is your friend. You could make him understand he'll never subdue the Navajo, that he'll have to kill them all if he keeps on with this."

"If I could have made him understand that — really understand it — I'd never have left his camp," Lindquist said quietly.

He smiled wryly. "Now I can't go back. I'd be shot, according to military law. A fair and square trial by court-martial, naturally. But stood up and shot, just the same."

"It's a bad thing, Rick!" Micaela said bitterly. "It's a terribly bad thing!"

"That part of it is," Lindquist agreed with an extension of his wryness.

"All of it is!" Micaela breathed.

Lindquist nodded. It was wrong, but it was also inescapable. And it was made no better by the fact that the military commandant was Colonel Kit Carson, the civilian-turned-soldier who had never suffered defeat at the hands of any Indians in a major engagement. Lindquist was grateful when the muffled sound of many horses racing across the sand came up the canyon. The main body of the horsemen and the loose animals they were driving went on past, heading deeper into the tortuous passages of de Chelly. Only Chief Juanito rode up to the place where Lindquist and Micaela were waiting.

The chief of the Navajo vaulted from the back of his mount and trotted toward them with the exuberance of a boy. He gripped Lindquist's arm with self-delighted enthusiasm.

"You got the guns?"

"A wagonload of them," Lindquist agreed. "How much hair did you lift up there on the rim?"

"We tricked the soldiers with the horses and disarmed them without trouble. The soldiers on the trail we drove to cover without harming one. As you said, we killed no Army men."

"We heard gunfire. What was it, a Ute attack from behind you?"

Juanito's eyes rounded with wicked, amused guilelessness.

"Utes, señor?" He shrugged elaborately. "There *were* some shadows, when I think of it. But it was very dark. Myself, I do not know. Some of my young men were nervous and feared it was an attack. There was a little shooting, but not much." He paused as though in careful thought. "It is possible there are a few dead Utes on the mesa. But who cares of this? Utes are not in uniform. They are not soldiers. They amount to less than nothing. They are Indians."

Lindquist did not miss the Indian's gentle irony. It was true that the military seldom showed concern for Indian casualties. But Carson's command would, this time.

"The Utes are Army scouts, Chief, officially attached," he said grimly. "My plan won't work now at all."

Juanito retained his grip on Lindquist's arm. He sobered, drawing on the immense reserve of dignity most leaders of the tribes seemed to possess. With the pressure of his hand he signaled Lindquist to sit back down and squatted near him.

"Hear the truth," he said. "Your plan would never have worked. I knew this from the beginning. Even a strong chief can keep his people from war only for a little time when an enemy comes among them."

"You agreed to give my plan a try!" Lindquist said sharply.

The Navajo nodded. He indicated Micaela.

"You and the woman have done much to help us. You are friends. We owed you something. The Council agreed with me. We did what we could."

"So you pretended to take my advice, but went right ahead with your own plans!" Exasperation roughened Lindquist's voice.

Juanito shrugged uncomfortably. "One fights a war the best way he can, señor."

This was fact. Lindquist accepted it as such.

"All right, what happens now?"

The Indian nodded off into the darkness. "The soldiers who were sent down to the mouth of the canyon have not had the trouble their friends have."

"Captain Carey's command?" Lindquist asked.

Juanito nodded. "They have traveled swiftly. They are camped just below the main trail. We had trouble slipping past them to the rim of the mesa and back down with the horses we captured there."

"It looks like the squeeze is beginning. Pfieffer's force is going to be after blood in the morning, after being disarmed and set afoot. It'll join Carey's command and move this way with it."

"I think so," Juanito agreed. "Orders have already been issued. Two hundred of my men will attack them from the canyon walls as soon as they start to move."

"You can't do anything that way!" Lindquist protested helplessly. "Carson has plenty of replacement equipment. The cavalrymen will be ten times as well armed as your men. They'll cut your two hundred to pieces!"

"It is expected we will lose these men," Juanito said quietly. "But it will cost the soldiers a little blood too. When it is done, they will think they've won a victory. But when they start to move again, another two hundred Navajo will attack from another place on the walls. It will be like that until there are no soldiers left. We have few guns, but we have many men."

"You know how this is going to end, don't you?"

Juanito nodded solemnly. "Against other Indians we would have victory. Among Indians we are many. Other tribes have never entered these canyons for that reason. They have come to the mesas a few times to steal our stock or careless women wandering too far from safety. But never into de Chelly itself. Among whites we are few. There will be more soldiers — always more soldiers — until there are no more Navajo. But this will take time — perhaps many months of time. And time is all that is left for us. We will fight for it!"

"You're crazy!" Lindquist said with conviction.

The Indian shrugged. "What would you do?"

"I told you already, but you paid no attention!"

"To a plan you knew would not work when you suggested it, señor. Who is really crazy?"

Juanito rose and crossed to his horse. He swung up, and without looking back he rode into the darkness toward the temporary headquarters across the canyon. He obviously expected Micaela and Lindquist to follow him afoot. Lindquist stared after him in uneasy speculation.

"He's tricky," he growled. "Smart, too. Anybody'd admit it, if his skin was a different color. He's got something up his sleeve."

"He told you his plans, Rick," Micaela pointed out.

"Not all of them," Lindquist corrected stubbornly. "He's not acting like a chief who knows his tribe is going to be wiped out and who is trying to make the best of it. Nobody makes the best of a thing like that. They take it hard. Juanito's not taking it hard enough to suit me."

"An Indian doesn't turn himself inside out so everybody can see how he thinks and feels, Rick."

"I know. But he doesn't make a joke out of losing his hair, either. I was watching Juanito close. He's happy about something."

"How could he be? If you're right about the Army not giving up until its orders are carried out to the letter, then the whole thing is hopeless and Juanito can see it as well as you or I can."

"He ought to. The point is, he doesn't. I'm afraid the crazy Indian believes he's got something left he can use in trade with Carson."

Micaela looked at him with total lack of understanding. Lindquist debated whether frightening her was worse than letting her face the truth.

"I think he's figuring on using you."

"Me?"

"I think so," Lindquist told her. "From an Indian point of view, whites have an important weak spot. The tribes have used it often enough too. Whites — particularly soldiers — will make some almighty damned-fool sacrifices for a woman. Not any woman — just a white woman. The younger she is and the prettier, the bigger the sacrifices. Juanito may have some ideas."

"About holding me as a hostage?"

"If his people could be saved by it, he'd use you for anything. We're not going to hang around and see just what his idea is!"

Micaela permitted him to steer her toward the foot of the trail on which Pfieffer's party had so recently been trapped. She turned as they reached the rock.

"Rick — Rick, I —"

"I know," Lindquist muttered. "That makes both of us fools. I guess I'd let Juanito use you, too, if it would save the tribe. But it won't, and I'm getting you out of his reach before he tries it, anyway!"

Micaela looked up at Lindquist in the darkness. He thought there was something else she wanted to say. But when she remained silent, he pushed her toward the worn steps cut into the wall before them.

The climb up the trail in the early-morning darkness was Lindquist's eeriest experience to date in this broken land of the unexpected and the unusual. It was easy to understand why even the hardened veterans in Captain Pfieffer's command had willingly surrendered their arms to escape their position after only a few hours of being marooned on the narrow, treacherous track.

Micaela, moving ahead of him, had a surety which came from familiarity with the trail and with such climbing, and he was grateful for her guidance and an occasional word of warning, passed back as they reached a difficult stretch. She climbed with what seemed to him amazing swiftness, yet pursuit from below overtook them before they reached the rim.

It was Micaela who discovered the half dozen knee-padded, half-naked figures moving in swift silence up a series of handholds they had themselves just traversed. She paused on a brief shelving, waited for Lindquist to reach her, and pointed downward to the Navajo. Lindquist's lips tightened. If he needed proof Juanito did in fact have use for the girl, this was it. He gestured for Micaela to work around a small outcropping which would give her shelter, and he drew his gun, keeping himself low so that the climbing Indians would not see their quarry had turned upon them.

He waited until the first man was within half a dozen yards of him. The Navajo's labored breathing was clearly audible. Certain the range was short enough for accuracy in the bad light, Lindquist fired. The bullet struck the Navajo in the head, and its downward force literally drove his body outward into space. It turned once freely and struck the second man. He cried out and slapped frantically for a new grip before sliding at rushing speed down the smooth sandstone into the darkness.

Lindquist leveled and fired again while the Indians, caught on the face of the open stone, clung precariously in indecision for a moment. The bullet went a little high, clearing the third man and ricocheting short of the fourth. The flattened, glancing slug struck the fourth man in the body. He slid limply from his position.

Realizing the ricochet improved accuracy, Lindquist calmly aimed short of the intervening man he had missed. Lead sang against stone and struck flesh. The remaining two Navajo frantically avoided the body as it tumbled toward them.

Range was greater now, the last two targets farther down. But the light was not so bad as Lindquist feared. He fired twice more, quite deliberately, and the bald face of the cliff was empty. He reloaded and recapped his gun. When he returned to Micaela, she asked no questions. They resumed their climb in silence.

Nearing the summit, Lindquist suddenly grabbed the girl and signaled for quiet. When she understood his caution, he slipped past her, taking care his own movements were soundless. Perhaps it was some sixth sense, perhaps only awareness the sound of his gun would have been readily audible here at the rim and so might have drawn attention. However it was, his caution proved wise. Just short of the last pitch he halted and flattened against the rock. Voices reached him. Guttural voices, speaking guardedly in the Ute dialect. He also heard horses, restlessly ground-tied. A lot of them. So there were a lot of the Utes also. Two of them seemed to be in a position almost directly over him.

"Big canyon makes many echoes," one of them growled. "The guns sounded close, but how many were there? Who knows? Who knows what was gun and what was echo? It is not for me to climb down and see about the shooting!"

"Nor for me," his companion agreed. "Tomorrow there will be enough shooting for us, anyway."

The first Ute chuckled with anticipation. He made a coarse comment about the Navajo. His companion laughingly boasted that the unhappiness of the Navajo women would shortly be over. Shortly they would begin to live. Tomorrow they would be prisoners of the Utes with Ute men about them. Tomorrow they would be Ute slaves. The two then fell to bantering as to which would lay hands on the best-looking Navajo squaw, and they moved away. There was considerable movement about the rim for a few more minutes, and Lindquist thought the Utes were seeing to the dead who had fallen to Juanito's earlier raiding party. Presently horses were mounted and the Indians departed.

Lindquist drew a short breath. He thought only a dozen Utes had been at the actual rim, but they had joined others farther back on the mesa. It was hard to tell how many there were, all told. A big party, for sure. Really big. A hundred, two hundred — maybe more. And they had ridden eastward, toward the head of Canyon de Chelly, where the weathering of the walls and the rising of the canyon itself offered many places of easy descent to the sand of its floor. He called softly to Micaela. She joined him in a moment and they started up the last pitch to the rim.

SEVENTEEN

Steve Grayson slept far more heavily than he intended. The camp was in a thorough uproar when he roused. It was dark. He didn't know how far into the night he had slept. Throwing back his blankets, he rolled out, forgetting about his nicked scalp until the fly of the tent brushed across it and stung him. As he started toward Colonel Carson's tent he encountered weary members of his own detachment, whom he had last seen riding toward the head of the foot trail into the canyon with Captain Pfieffer. The captain was prominent in the group before Carson's tent. Pfieffer seemed to be in a bad humor, and the two or three troopers to whom Grayson spoke gave him only a surly stare for answer. He was almost across to Carson's quarters before he realized something was markedly amiss with Pfieffer's men. They bore no arms.

Colonel Carson showed evidence of having also been soundly asleep when Pfieffer's party returned. He was without his shirt. His hair was tousled. And he kept massaging one eye as Pfieffer stalked back and forth in front of him with short, jerky pacing, delivering a somewhat incredulous report with a remarkable profanity. Carson, aside from rubbing his one eye, made no attempt to hide the considerable amusement which gripped him. By the time he had sorted out Pfieffer's profane personal asides from the meat of his report, Grayson had recovered from the shock of realizing a competent detachment of seasoned military men had been completely disarmed by a few savages, and the humor of the situation began to appeal to him also. It was regrettable he didn't have a colonel's insignia to protect him so that he could also enjoy it openly.

"I request permission to re-equip immediately and return to an engagement with the hostiles, sir," Pfieffer said. "I have been made a fool. Every man in my command has been made a fool. I won't take it!"

"These things happen, Captain," Carson said, still rubbing his eye.

"When?" Pfieffer demanded. "When did a thing like this ever happen? Forty men disarmed without ever firing a shot!"

"Well, now that you mention it," Carson agreed with a grin, "now that you mention it, I don't know as it ever did happen before. A very unique experience, Captain."

"Unique!" Pfieffer was in an agony of repression. Grayson enjoyed it thoroughly, remembering his own discomfort at the captain's hands when he had believed himself a casualty. "Unique! By God, sir, it's the damnedest thing I ever heard of! And the sooner I've got my hooks into those Navajo, the better I'll like it. I speak for every man in my detachment too! Wait till one of us has that renegade Lindquist in his sights. Just once is all we need!"

"Lindquist?" Carson said gently. "Lindquist is attached to this command."

"He's with the Navajo!"

"Well, he's sure enough absent from the command without leave, but are you sure he had anything to do with this business on the canyon wall?"

"Sure? We heard him. It was his idea. No Indian's that smart!"

"I'm afraid Lindquist will have to answer for this, then."

"He will!" Pfieffer promised. "He will. Wait and see. Do I have permission to order my men out as soon as they've re-equipped?"

"It's been my observation, Captain, that sleepy men do not fight well."

"Angry ones do, and my men are sore as hell!"

"Order them to their billets for four hours, Captain. They need rest. I will send a courier to Captain Carey, advising him we will join him in strength, just short of daybreak." Carson turned and pointed the finger with which he had been rubbing his eye at Grayson. "Lieutenant, I am ordering out the Utes encamped on the bench above us. Their instructions will be to see to their dead in the vicinity of the point where Captain Pfieffer lost his horses. Having done this, they are to move up the south rim of the canyon to such a point as they can enter it with ease. Achieving this, they are to work back down the floor of the canyon, cutting off any possibility of a Navajo retreat in that direction."

"Yes, sir," Grayson said.

"You will accompany them to the head of the foot trail and make certain that getting upset over their dead there doesn't make them attempt the foot trail. You are charged with this responsibility. Once they have started on up along the rim, you are to report back to me here."

"Yes, sir," Grayson said again.

Carson smiled with considerable friendliness and turned back into his tent. Pfieffer, face set as grimly as the stone of de Chelly, stalked back through the camp.

Grayson, without intending to do so, found himself in step beside the captain. There seemed some obligation to say something. Grayson tried.

"Rotten luck, sir," he suggested.

Pfieffer turned on him like a tiger.

"There's nothing I can do while we're operating out here so far from a normal chain of command, Grayson!" he snapped. "I'm not fool enough to expect anything from Colonel Carson. But when we're back on an Army reservation with Army command to deal with, I'm demanding an explanation of why you failed to deliver my report and request to Carson with sufficient urgency to have persuaded him to send me support when I needed it. You'd better have that explanation and it had better be good!"

Pfieffer bent and entered his tent. Grayson fingered the crease on the side of his head for a moment and shrugged. It sort of seemed like things were going to hell, and he wasn't just sure why.

A Ute scout came down from Carson's tent and signaled to Steve. He angled over to the remount pickets and indicated a likely horse. The pickets saddled the animal. The Ute was already up. Grayson crossed to him, and the two of them rode into the timber on the mesa side of the camp.

A quarter of a mile from headquarters, Grayson and his Indian guide came on a mass of Utes, mounted and waiting in utter silence in the timbered shadows. Grayson was startled. This was an efficient military force, prepared and held in readiness. For all the casualness of Carson's orders to him, it appeared the colonel had made preparations for even the contingency facing him now. Certainly the Utes had been alerted before any word of Pfieffer's debacle on the canyon wall could have reached the main camp. Grayson found himself wondering just how far Carson's anticipatory strategy reached. He glumly concluded that he, as well as some others, might well be underestimating the shrewdness of their commander.

His Ute companion relayed Carson's commands to the Ute company. Grayson had no way of knowing if the orders were correctly translated. He wondered if his presence was sufficient to ensure that the Indians carried out the orders as issued. He assumed this was the case. Otherwise Carson would have taken other precautions. But this ride was a thankless one.

A man fought fire with fire. An eye for an eye and a tooth for a tooth was a well enough established principle. Nevertheless, there was something offensive in employing savage allies to overcome a savage enemy. It sort of reflected on the effectiveness of the United States Army — a kind of self-admission that cavalry forces in de Chelly were insufficient for the task assigned to them. He regretted the Utes were on the mesa. He wanted to be done with them as swiftly as possible.

As he rode, however, he was forced to an admiration of the party he accompanied. They moved in almost complete silence. They moved swiftly. And in their silence was a remarkable feeling of strength and competence. Perhaps a quarter of a mile from the shelf on the lip of the mesa where the foot trail into the canyon headed out, they emerged from timber into a small meadow, and an Indian on the flank of the party called out sharply. The whole group wheeled and centered on him. Sprawled in a small area were the bodies of half a dozen of their kind.

Dispersal of the bodies indicated this had been a small foraging party out looking for trouble. They certainly had found it. Chief Juanito's raiders from the canyon floor, closing in on Pfieffer's horses, had apparently come suddenly on this Ute party. The condition of the bodies indicated they had been caught in a Navajo cross fire. There had been no chance for them. This must also be apparent to Grayson's Ute companions, but they accepted the dead calmly. Two or three dismounted and began loading the dead across the backs of their own horses, three bodies to an animal. Another small group reined off toward the head of the trail. Grayson felt obliged to accompany them, since the colonel's orders had been that none of the Utes attempt descent of the trail.

Nearly to the rim, gun sound rose from the void of the canyon, beyond it. The ricochet of sound from the walls made identification difficult, but Grayson thought the fire was all from one gun — five shots measured off in brief, nearly equal intervals, like a careful man making sure of a like number of targets. Two of the Utes dismounted and moved to the head of the trail. They talked briefly there, made a joke between them, and moved back to Grayson and their companions.

The Ute who had been his guide from headquarters signaled that he and his fellows were returning to join their main party in the meadow and that they would continue on along the rim toward the head of the canyon. Grayson nodded. The Indians withdrew, joined the others, and the lot of them faded off up-country. Grayson breathed a little easier, accepting this as proof the colonel's instructions had been carried out. There remained only an urge to efficiency which required an investigation of his own of the gunfire they had heard from below. After this he could return to Carson's camp.

He rode as close as practicable to the head of the foot trail, dismounted, and approached the beginning of the chipped downward steps afoot. Just short of them, he froze in his tracks. Sound of ascent came up the wall. He quietly drew his gun and crouched low against the ground to avoid silhouette. The sound was not loud. Whoever was climbing was cautious. A head appeared over the rim and Grayson grunted involuntarily in surprise. The head belonged to Micaela Castaneda.

The girl heard his sharp explosion of breath and glanced nervously about, crouching on the rock. Grayson had an honest respect for her skill with a gun, but he doubted the weapon he had heard firing down on the wall had been in her hand. He was certain someone else climbed with her. And he thought he knew who it was. His hand gripped the butt of his pistol more tightly. Micaela's searching eyes picked out his shadow.

"Un soldado!" she cried with unnecessary loudness. "Mother of mercy, a soldier!"

She sprang to her feet at the head of the trail and ran straight toward Grayson. He side-stepped a little, seeing movement behind her, but she veered and ran straight into him, her arms wide-swept. Grayson tried frantically to disengage himself, but the girl clung desperately. He wheeled almost completely about, trying to throw her off, and while his back was momentarily turned quarteringly, another figure plowed into them. A powerful, leather-clad arm reached over his shoulder to lock under his chin. Another shot under his arm, and steel fingers clamped on the wrist of his gun hand. Muscle ridges across a wide chest pressed against his shoulder blades, and although he put every ounce of his own angry weight into resistance, his gun hand was dragged behind him and forced up into the small of his back, and as the joints of his elbow and shoulder began to spring from their sockets under the brutal pressure, the gun spilled helplessly from his fingers.

The pressure was instantly released. He was shoved away from his assailant so violently he stumbled awkwardly. When he regained his balance and wheeled, Eric Lindquist stood panting beside Micaela, holding his own gun in one hand and Grayson's in the other.

"Sorry, Steve," Lindquist said in a tone of surprising earnestness. "Seems like you and me've had to do all the fighting in this war, so far."

"We're going to do some more!" Grayson promised bitterly.

"It'll have to wait," Lindquist said. "You with the Utes that were up here?"

"Sure," Grayson told him grimly. "You were in a little too much hurry, Lindquist. They haven't pulled out yet. How do you like that bunch standing over there?"

He tilted his head casually. He did a good job of it. He caught Lindquist completely off guard. The leather man turned slightly to look in the indicated direction. Grayson lunged at him. Lindquist swung back too late to avoid the impact. They went down together. Lindquist was a powerful man, but Steve Grayson was angry, outraged, vindictively righteous.

Lindquist was a traitor to his flag and his kind. In his fury Steve forgot the guns in Lindquist's hands. He forgot the small matter of the difference in their size. He wanted blood and he went after it.

As they hit the stone underfoot, he had Lindquist's throat. With this hold he banged the leather man's head against stone. He walked on his knees from Lindquist's groin to his breastbone, bearing down with sharp, stabbing pressure which drove hurt sounds from the man under him. He freed one hand and hit Lindquist in the face with considerable more effectiveness than he anticipated. He heard one of the guns skitter across rock, escaping from his enemy. He closed his fingers again on Lindquist's throat and took half a dozen explosive, close-range drives of the man's free hand to his belly in exchange for the privilege of shutting off Lindquist's air — permanently, he hoped.

Lindquist threshed frantically and they rolled, but Grayson clung to his grip. His lips were back from his teeth. His breath was whistling, but Lindquist wasn't breathing. He couldn't. And a wicked elation was up in Grayson. When man quit fighting his wars with his hands and took to weapons, a great satisfaction had been lost.

They rolled again, and Grayson struggled to emerge once more atop his foe, clinging to the initial advantage of the surprise with which he had charged. As he straightened in an attempt to increase the clamping pressure of his fingers, his back stiffened into something hard and prodding against his spine. And Micaela's voice, sobbing, was in his ears.

"Lieutenant, please — please!"

He tried to look at her but was afraid to take his eyes from the darkening face of the man under him. He heard the pistol she held against him come to cock.

"Please, Lieutenant, I don't want to shoot!"

"Get away!" Grayson grunted. "Get away, you little fool!"

"Please . . ." The sob was gone from Micaela's voice. It was steady. So was the pressure of the gun. And Grayson had a sudden anticipation of what a bullet at this range would do to the bones of a man's spine. His fingers relaxed. He hunched and sprang suddenly upward, wheeling to catch the girl. But she was wary. She darted back a pair of steps, holding the gun low and ready. Tears were streaming down her face as though it had broken her heart to threaten his life.

"Thank you . . ." she whispered. But she held the gun very steady and her finger was tight against the trigger. The gun waggled a little in an order. Grayson moved with reluctant obedience. The girl also moved, circling toward Lindquist, who had risen to a sitting position. He was chafing his throat. He looked up at Grayson.

"Christ!" he said unsteadily, and he climbed to his feet. He still held his own gun in his hand, and Grayson belatedly realized the man could have fired it into his attacker's body at any time during their struggle. He began to feel a little weak in the middle. Lindquist wiped his hand across a swollen lump on his jaw and restored his gun to its holster.

"Those Utes —" he said to the girl. "They were heading east — there were a lot of them. I've got to trail them. I'll take Steve's horse. He'll get you back to Carson's camp. All right?"

"You're going back with us!" Grayson said without conviction.

Lindquist shook his head. "You take care of her." He turned to the girl. "You don't know anything about what's happening in the canyon. Not anything. Remember?"

Micaela nodded. Moving stiffly, Lindquist crossed to Grayson's horse. Grayson watched him go with a feeling of complete helplessness. There was also a feeling he had made a complete fool of himself, but he couldn't quite see how. And he had some consolation. Lindquist was only escaping temporarily. Sooner or later he'd be up against the rifles of Carson's troopers. Or maybe the guns of the Utes up the canyon. And one of them would finish the job he had started here in the canyon.

When Lindquist was out of sight Grayson reached out his hand. Micaela surrendered his gun to him.

"You did a good thing, Estevan. A wonderfully good thing!"

"Yeah!" Grayson said.

"Believe me!" Micaela begged. "Believe me, it's true. I — I am grateful."

Grayson let down the hammer of his gun and holstered it.

"Yeah!" he said again.

Micaela gripped his arms and looked up into his face.

"It is true, Estevan. I am very grateful."

Grayson considered this. He let his hands slide along her arms to her shoulders and he pulled her to him. Her face remained upturned. He kissed her. With no particular gentleness, either. And for a long time. She remained in his arms and she kissed him. Grayson released her finally.

"I'm damned!" he said.

"What's the matter?"

"I'm still in one piece. Come on, let's get back to camp."

EIGHTEEN

It took a quarter of a mile of hard riding after the Ute party for Lindquist to regain normal breathing. And the hackles on the back of his neck were about as long in flattening. Steve Grayson had been out for his life and he knew it. If it had not been for Micaela, there would have been a dead mountain man or a dead lieutenant on the rim of the mesa. Lindquist was very grateful for the girl's intervention. There was only one thing about it he didn't like. At first he thought she had launched herself at Grayson to save Eric Lindquist's life.

But there had been tears in her eyes when she held a cocked gun on Grayson and she had been almighty soft in her thanks to the cavalryman when Lindquist was back on his feet. And there was the matter of a silhouette which appeared as one body, rather than two, which had been visible on the rim of the mesa when Lindquist looked back before riding into the timber after the Utes. He supposed the girl felt obliged to make her peace with Grayson, but this was a thing which could be overdone. It was a hell of a note when a man had something he wanted to get straightened out with a woman and then didn't have time to get to it. Lindquist growled about this as he rode until he remembered he had had plenty of time in the early hours of the night to straighten out anything he wanted with Micaela — and nobody around to interrupt, either. It was his fault. No doubt of that. He just didn't get to it. And he had no right to resent Grayson because of it. He knew this, but he felt no better for it.

The Utes ahead of him were riding at a reckless speed. Lindquist was even more reckless in his attempt to overtake them, riding as fast as he could drive Grayson's horse for five minutes, then halting briefly to listen for sound of the Indians ahead of him — the only precaution he could take to avoid riding full into them unawares. It was half an hour before he picked up the sound of the Utes ahead. He slowed a little then, matching his speed to theirs. And he grinned a little at an anticipated and typical Indian peculiarity.

Probably no people on the face of the earth were able to move individually with such skillful silence as the men of the mountain tribes. The Utes were especially

271

adept at stalking. But now that they were in full cry after their quarry, the bunch ahead of him had abandoned silence and seemed to be careless of sound in direct proportion to the size of their group. One Indian could climb into your pocket without being heard. Ten could pass within as many feet. But the progress of a hundred could be heard half a mile away.

It was just as well. Lindquist made certain the Utes maintained a substantial lead on him. He had no desire to run into them. He wanted merely to follow them. They were obviously bent on a particular piece of business. He wanted to know what it was.

Time passed, with the Utes heading steadily into the east, widely skirting small, deeply cut side canyons which fed into de Chelly. He dropped farther behind them as false dawn drove back the deep night shadows and visibility became something with which to reckon. The Utes, silhouetted in the magnificence inevitable when a hundred horsemen of any race rode together, passed over a low rise a mile ahead and dropped into a depression beyond a few moments before the body of the sun rose with explosive suddenness over the mesas.

Lindquist swung through a rough area of broken stone and found himself at the head of a brief, stiff pitch too flattened to be called a wall. At the foot of this was the sandy, narrowing ribbon which was the floor of the upper end of the great canyon of the Navajo.

Winding along this in the absolute silence of desperation was something which explained many things. In the first place, here was the target of the Utes — here was their quarry. And here, too, was the last trick Chief Juanito and the old men of the Navajo Council had held back from Micaela and himself. This — not a menace to the Spanish girl — was the reason why the Navajo chief had retained a hope for the salvation of his people, even in the face of Lindquist's assertion that only the alternatives of surrender or destruction lay before them. Here was the thing Carson must have anticipated with all the shrewdness characteristic of the man. Otherwise the Utes would not have been dispatched in this direction in strength.

Here was something on a scale Rick Lindquist — for all his years in the mountains — had never seen equaled. Perhaps because the movement below him was something even history did not often encounter. An entire nation was in motion on the tiny ribbon of sand.

First came mounted and armed men. A compact party of them, flanked by outriders who combed every shelter and variation along the canyon floor to be certain the way was clear for those behind. Next came the stock. Horses by the hundreds, sheep by the thousands, even a few cattle. And numberless dogs milling about the mass, aiding in the drive, but now strangely as silent as their masters. Behind this double wall of mounted warriors and massed animals came the women and the children and the aged. Among these were travois litters trailing behind single ponies and a number of the big-wheeled, clumsy carts in which the Spanish had rolled up out of Mexico onto the high desert. Behind the *carretas* came a smaller rear-guard phalanx of fighting men, afoot.

Dust hung over the whole cavalcade. Dust and silence. By far the greatest mass was in the center — the women, the old, the very young. Lindquist realized Juanito and the Council had spared only enough warriors to provide the immense exodus with reasonable protection. The balance had been held far down the canyon to buy time for these with their lives.

The Navajo strategy was immediately clear. If the nation was to move to new quarters, it was not to be at Bosque Redondo, under the orders of the Army and the government, but to a place of its own choice. They were moving eastward now, but once free of the confines of the canyon, they could swing north and back into the west. In this direction lay the great desert. Between the upper reaches of the Rio Grande and San Juan rivers and the chasms of the Colorado was a huge area of emptiness, completely unknown to the *yanqui*. It had been uncrossed as far as Lindquist knew by even the most curious of the mountain men. Here a nation could vanish. This, rather than reservation imprisonment, was the Navajo choice.

It was a stubborn kind of bravery, but it was bravery, nevertheless. A defiant courage which commanded respect. Lindquist understood fully now how Micaela Castaneda and her father could have lost everything they owned to these people and still remain loyal to them. Something of the incredibility and magnificence which was the country about de Chelly belonged also to the Navajo. If there were affection and loyalty for this country, then there must be affection and loyalty for its people also.

Suddenly Lindquist recognized the elusive thing he had found here — the thing he could not identify. The something which was partly desire for the Spanish girl Steve Grayson's handsomeness and youth and bright uniform had taken from him, and partly something else. A man moved from one place to another because of restlessness. And restlessness was a hunting, as a man hunted for food. A hunting within himself or for a country or for a woman. He kept on moving, living with his restlessness, until he found what he wanted or he died. Lindquist knew he would have to hunt no farther. Here was the country. A place for a tall man to strike down his roots where his kind had not been before.

He remembered his talk with Steve Grayson on the rim of the mesa, waiting for another dawn. Talk of seasons and grazing and cattle, of canyons and mesas. The land was for the taking. What could be built upon it lay in the strength of a man's hands, his patience, and the depths of his convictions.

Suddenly Lindquist's concern for the Navajo, which had baffled him no less than it had obviously baffled the Indians themselves, took on clear shape and meaning.

Like the great red sandstone of de Chelly, the Navajo belonged here. The mesas would be incomplete without them. An army could not move the mountains and drive the mesas away and fill in the deep channels of the canyons. An army could not erase the Navajo from the country of their gods, either.

A distant shout broke the spell of the thing Lindquist had seen. The shout swelled into ululations, and the Utes he had been trailing broke from shelter to pour into the canyon. They spread out, blocking the Navajo advance. The two forces measured each other warily. Then the Utes began to advance. It was immediately clear to Lindquist that the Navajo had sufficient strength to protect themselves so long as they could give ground, but that they didn't have enough fighting men to drive a safe passage for the whole huge caravan through the barricading Ute force.

The Navajo leaders below seemed to reach the same conclusion almost as swiftly. With their women, children, stock, and possessions to protect, they began a slow and orderly retreat back down the canyon as the Utes put skirmishing pressure against them. Lindquist watched a few moments in a kind of helpless fascination, knowing one man could do nothing to alter the balance below. And as he watched, the intention of the Utes — or the nature of their orders from Carson — became clear.

They could no more drive into the Navajo without prohibitive cost than the Navajo could cut through them. But they could maintain sufficient pressure to force a steady Navajo retreat. It was therefore only a question of time until Carson's cavalrymen, working up the canyon against Juanito's delaying forces, would catch the body of the nation in a vise and the Utes would be able to claim their share of the captives at little cost.

There was only one thing to do. Lindquist put his startled horse down the steep slope before him. Slipping, clattering, more sliding than running, the frantic animal kept its feet under it only by a miracle. Lindquist hit the canyon floor a mile below the vanguard of the retreating Navajo. A few desultory shots were fired after him, but the range was much too great for the miserable smoothbore Spanish muskets most of the de Chelly men possessed. Leaning low over the neck of his horse, Lindquist lifted it to a frantic run down the canyon.

★ ★ ★

The sun was brassily hot wherever its ray struck squarely down between the vertical walls of the canyon. Grayson was sweating, his face streaked and the underarms of his shirt wet to the waist. And he felt a little sick. The firing had almost died. Here and there a trooper, striving for dead-sureness, loosed a settling shot at one of the sprawled bodies heaped on the sand near the mouth of a small side fissure in the north canyon wall. Pfieffer and Carey had fallen back to speak briefly with the colonel. Carey returned, hugging the south wall as though an enemy unit still faced him. He signaled to his sergeants, and the cease-fire order went out. Grayson piled from the rocks where he'd been stationed and started out across the sandy canyon floor toward the sprawl of enemy casualties.

The first time he had to do this, his skin crawled the whole way and with every step he had waited for a bullet from the gun of some die-hard Navajo who had escaped the withering fire poured into the Navajo position. This first time had been half a mile down the canyon, nearly an hour ago. When he reached the Navajo dead, he understood why he had not been fired upon.

No Indians had remained alive.

Now he walked easily. This second group of Indians had attacked the column exactly as hard as the first, and apparently in about the same strength. Exchange of fire had been equally as heated and had lasted about as long. It had ended in the same way — with no further defense from the Indian position. Acutely conscious of the heat and the smell of blood and the grotesqueness of the sprawled bodies of the Navajo dead, Grayson moved through them, making a quick count — appraising the quality of weapons and the apparent ammunition supply.

He was about to turn back when a sound came from the bodies which had spilled down from the crevices in which this group had been holed up. Turning back, fighting his own stomach afresh, he rolled the body of an old man aside. A boy lay in the sand, hands clamped over a huge hole in his chest. Lead ricocheting from stone often made such a wound. The boy was dying and he was in agony. The sound came from the grinding of his tightly clamped teeth. He looked up at Grayson with open, defiant eyes. But there was appeal in them.

Grayson coughed a little, choking, and tried to turn away but found he could not.

He wondered how the boy had ever been able to sight one of the muskets protruding from the heap of bodies. He wondered how a boy had been included by the Indians in this group of men. He remembered a brassy recruitment sergeant in his own training days who had boasted that boys made better soldiers than men. This one had been a good soldier. He drew his sidearm and started to put it down within the boy's reach, but he realized he was being a bigger fool and more of a coward than the dying young Indian. He sighted quickly and fired. Gratitude flashed in the boy's suffering eyes, and the lids dropped. Grayson wished they had closed completely. He put the gun back into its holster and stumbled across the sand toward the command.

Pfieffer and Carey were with the colonel. Carson looked up, saw something in Grayson's face, and dismissed the other two officers. The colonel was squatting over a tiny fire in the shade of a big boulder, boiling water in an incredibly battered little trail pot. He motioned Grayson to the sand beside him. Grayson sank down gratefully and watched Carson drop a few flakes of brittle tea into the pot.

The colonel was a hard man to figure.

Drinking gunpowder-laced whiskey in the leisure of his own camp and tea in the heat of battle. Carson looked up from his pot.

"Tea?" he asked.

Grayson took off his campaign hat and wiped his forehead with his kerchief for answer. Carson pulled the drawstring of the little pouch from which he had taken the tea and restored it to his shirt front. He poured a little brew from the pot into an equally battered issue cup, eyed the color, and, seemingly satisfied, poured the cup full. He pushed it toward Grayson.

"It'll cool you quicker'n ice if you drink it hot," he said. "Makes you sweat more, and evaporation does the trick. Seems crazy, but it's a fact. A Frenchman taught me."

Grayson shook his head.

Carson shrugged and picked up his cup. "One of those bullies over there try to nail you?" he asked. "They ought to have been all dead."

"They were — except this boy," Grayson said, living harshly through the experience all over again. "There — there wasn't anything else I could do for him."

"That takes guts, son," Carson murmured. "What's the casualty report?"

"The first attack, down the canyon, there

were about two hundred Navajo in the party. Five of our men were wounded with arrows, two dead of bullets."

"And the hostiles?"

"Between ten and twenty retreated afoot up the canyon, most of them wounded."

"And this attack here?"

"About two hundred Navajo again, sir. Eleven troopers wounded by gunfire, none seriously. One man killed by a falling rock — thrown by the enemy, I think. Sergeant Mollar killed by an arrow. One wounded hostile was captured, but he killed himself. Half a dozen or so retreated again. No other survivors over there."

Carson wiped his mustache. "You make a good report, Lieutenant. When a war's got a shooting stage, it's kind of hard to sit to one side and see all that's happening and make a count of who's hit and the like. And you got sand to make a count of enemy casualties. Nobody can tell when an Indian's playing possum. I'll see you're mentioned."

"Thank you, sir," Grayson said rigidly. He glared at Carson as the colonel swilled off the balance of his tea. There was little wonder the man had the reputation he did. Nothing fazed him. Absolutely nothing. That, or he didn't understand that the two attacks they'd weathered this morning were nothing to what lay ahead of them.

"With the colonel's permission, sir . . . ?" he said.

Carson put the cup down. "Son, if you were to bend of a sudden, you'd bust in two! This is no time to keep a ramrod down your collar. If you've got something to say, why, up and say it!"

"Yes, sir," Grayson said. He leaned earnestly forward. "Chief Juanito is holding us up the best way he can — deliberately fighting for time for some reason or another. Every time we start moving up this canyon we're going to get hit by one of these suicide attacks — just enough men thrown at us to stop us cold till we wipe them out. Juanito can keep this up till he's run out of men — and he's got a lot of them!"

"He sure has," Carson agreed tranquilly. "More than enough to wipe us out to the last man if he'd toss them at us all at once. Supposing you tell me why he doesn't do that and be done with it."

"I don't know."

Carson picked up a double handful of sand and dumped it on his tiny fire, quenching it. When he seemed satisfied no spark lingered, he rose to his feet. Grayson rose with him.

"You're going to make a tolerable Indian fighter," Carson said. "You read sign right good. And you know when you're stumped. Now, suppose you tell me where Rick Lindquist is."

"Lindquist!" Grayson's voice shook in spite of himself. "There's no doubt of where he is at all, sir! He's on up this canyon somewhere, egging more of these Navajo into getting themselves killed!"

Carson shook his head. "Getting killed isn't practical. These stalling attacks aren't Rick's idea, I'm sure of that. He'd have no part of this. He isn't with Juanito. He's someplace else. I want to find out where. Find the Castaneda girl and bring her up here. She didn't know anything about what was going on in the canyon or what Rick was up to when he left you last night. I don't mind a woman lying to me when I've got time on my hands and it's just me and her — but not when I've got a war on my hands!"

Grayson saluted and moved back through the troopers of the recombined command scattered along the narrow band of shade at the base of the canyon wall. Micaela and her father were talking to Captain Pfieffer. All three seemed angry, Pablo Castaneda perhaps even more so than the other two. Grayson realized he was interrupting and perhaps intruding, but he was operating under orders.

"Colonel Carson wants to see you, Micaela."

"Of course, Estevan," the girl said. She took his arm with a venomous backward glance at Pfieffer, who in turn glanced uneasily at the girl's father and moved briskly back toward his own men.

"The colonel's in a bad mood toward you, Micaela," Grayson warned. "If he starts getting a little rough with you, don't say anything. Leave it to me."

"Argh!" the girl snorted. "He can't be any worse than Captain Pfieffer!" She softened and smiled a little at Grayson. "If it wasn't for you, Estevan, I'd believe all *yanqui* soldiers think a uniform is an excuse for anything!"

Micaela was genuinely angry. Grayson thought it required no stretch of the imagination to guess what had disturbed her. Pfieffer, with his captaincy, had before now not been above using rank to requisition something in the possession of a junior officer if it struck his fancy. Grayson made a mental note to request the colonel's permission for a personal discussion with Captain Pfieffer on the conduct of an officer and a gentleman when this was over.

The captain seemed unable even to inquire the time of day without a military brusqueness which was irritating enough to his juniors, let alone to a girl who had little enough love for the military, anyway. For Pfieffer's own good he should be told that even the most efficient officer in the world couldn't successfully handle an attractive woman as though she was a drunken corporal or a green sentry caught dozing on duty. And then there was always the possibility Pfieffer had gone a little farther than this. Micaela was considerably more than merely attractive, and most men — even martinet officers — were human.

Carson rose with surprising grace when they arrived. He made a place for Micaela beside him and sat down again. This rather pointedly left Grayson standing, but since he was not dismissed, he remained.

"Now, look, honey," Carson said earnestly. "We've got a serious problem on our hands and you've got a bad memory. I've got a notion that if we could cure one we might cure the other. Try remembering where Rick Lindquist is — where he said he was going."

"We've been over that, *Coronel*," Micaela answered steadily.

"We've been through a couple of pretty nasty skirmishes since breakfast too," Carson said. "We'll go through more of them unless I can get in touch with Lindquist."

He paused and pointed across the canyon to where the sand was littered with the bodies of fallen Navajo. He swung back to the girl.

"You want us to have to keep that up, clear to the head of the canyon?"

Micaela's lips compressed. "But why Rick Lindquist? What can he do?"

"Talk to the Navajo, pound the truth into their skulls. Make them understand there's only one way out for them. I've been counting on him for that. He's let me down. I've got to find him!"

For the first time Grayson could feel urgency in Carson's manner. Micaela's eyes widened, but her astonishment was no greater than Grayson's own.

"You — you've been *counting* on Rick?" she repeated.

Carson nodded and smiled briefly.

"Even on you — for what you could do, honey," he agreed blandly. "You don't think either one of you could have escaped from my camp if I didn't have reason for seeing you had the opportunity to do so, do you?"

Grayson stared at his senior commander with utter incredulity.

"You mean Lindquist escaped from your camp with your — your —"

"Connivance, Lieutenant? No. Opportunity's still the better word. I figured opportunity was about all Rick would need, once I'd gotten him mad enough."

"But what in heaven's name could he do?"

"Help me carry out my orders, son. That's what you and the rest of those soldier boys are here for too. This isn't the easiest chore a man ever tackled. I figured Rick might do things for himself when he was steamed up that he wouldn't do for me or the Army of the United States, either one. And things had to be done."

"Then the two of you had a plan worked out all along!"

"Just me," Carson said with becoming modesty. "Rick thinks he's a fugitive, wanted for aiding the enemy. That's what he is — what he will be if we catch him too. But I've got to know where he is and what he's doing, just the same. He'll be trying as hard to stop this slaughter as we are. And he's the only one who can do it."

Grayson retreated from the conversation. It was altogether too much for him. He could recollect no evidence that Carson was now or ever had been trying to prevent extinction of the Navajo. But what he was beginning to see was Rick Lindquist's position from the very first. Carson was calmly using a man who had been his friend in some kind of subterfuge to entrap the Navajo. And the colonel was fast enough on his feet so that however it came out Lindquist was still going to have hold of the dirty end of the stick.

Grayson remembered his own initial feeling of close friendship for the tall mountain man and he was beginning to suspect he had been far too hasty in turning against Rick Lindquist. Anger stirred in him and he faced Carson grimly.

"I think Miss Castaneda has told us all she knows of Lindquist's whereabouts, sir. I suggest I be permitted to return her to her father."

Micaela looked at him a moment and slowly shook her head.

"No, Estevan," she said quietly. "Not yet. There is a little more to tell. You remember what Rick said as he left. He was following the Utes. He had to know what they were doing."

"The Utes?" Carson grunted.

"Yes, sir," Grayson said. "He followed them."

"Then he's clean to the top of the canyon — too far away from us. And somebody's got to talk to these Indians before they kill themselves all off and us with them!"

"I could try," Micaela offered.

"Read minds, don't you, honey?" Carson grinned at her. He sobered. "I don't know. They're worked up to a pretty high pitch. No telling what they'll do. I don't even know if the chief is down at this end of the canyon. The Utes are closing in from above on my orders. He may have word of that and be up there someplace with Lindquist now. Maybe we can't get to him. But we've got to try."

Grayson stirred decisively. "You can't send a woman out to face that next bunch of Navajo. We know they're there — up the canyon someplace — tense as drumheads, waiting for our next move."

"You've got it all wrong, Lieutenant," Carson said with sudden iron in his voice. "Maybe you can't send a woman out there, but I can. That's my job. I can do anything that will end this campaign at the least cost, including the risking of one life to save a great many lives. Escort Miss Castaneda within hailing distance of the next group of hostiles, then withdraw and permit her to proceed alone!"

Carson's manner made it clear this was an unquestionable order. Grayson made a swift decision and took his career in his hands.

"I can't permit it, sir!"

Carson looked at him in open astonishment.

Micaela spoke quickly. "Thank you, Estevan. But this time it is not for you to say. I'm ready, *Coronel*."

Carson pushed his hat onto the back of his head.

"I wish I had that general at Leavenworth who thought this campaign up right here with me about now!" he growled. "All right, honey. Get to Juanito somehow. These Indians were your neighbors. They've got to let you through. Tell the chief I've got to talk to him. Tell him I'll meet him wherever he says — alone."

As Micaela and Grayson started to turn away, Carson called as though in afterthought:

"You might tell Juanito he's boxed in,

too, just in case he hasn't spotted the Utes working down the canyon. It just might make him more reasonable all of a sudden."

NINETEEN

A quarter of a mile above the cavalry position Grayson tried to stop Micaela and
reason with her. She pulled away and kept
going, trudging in the soft footing of the
sand. He overtook her.

"I've got to talk to you a minute!" he
protested.

"We can talk while we're walking," she
said. "That way the Navajo will know we
know what we're doing — that we aren't
afraid."

"Aren't you — aren't you afraid?"

The girl shot him a quick glance over her
shoulder.

"Scared to death," she admitted. "But
we don't dare let the Indians know it. If we
show any uncertainty, they'll think we're
up to some kind of a trick."

"But we are, and they'll know it anyhow.
The minute we're in range, they'll start
shooting."

"Maybe not."

"I don't want you shot!" Grayson said in
an agony of concern.

"No? Why? You're a soldier, aren't you?

People are always getting shot around soldiers."

Micaela was being no help to him. Grayson suffered acutely. Finally he leaped.

"I'll tell you why I don't want you shot — why you mustn't go any farther. I — I love you!"

Micaela stopped in her tracks, forgetting her claim they had to keep moving steadily to allay Navajo suspicion. She stopped and turned and stared at Grayson with all sorts of mixed-up emotions on her face so that he had no way at all of measuring her reaction.

"I love you to beat the devil!" he added. And he realized his voice sounded angry. Matter of fact, he was angry. This was a hell of a place and a hell of a way to propose to a girl. He didn't even have his dress sword and a clean uniform on. And he smelled of sweat.

Micaela started to say something, all round-eyed and moist-lipped, but smoke blossomed behind a heap of boulders up the canyon behind her. The flat report of a rifle echoed against the canyon walls. Not the heavy whoop of a Navajo smoothbore, but a good Army rifle. Likely one of the guns taken from Pfieffer the night before. And the Indian behind its sights could shoot. Sand geysered up, spraying both the girl and himself.

She started and came within reach. Grayson grabbed her and pulled her to him. He started to kiss her, but the gun spoke again and fresh sand stung them. She broke away.

"Go back, Estevan! They are shooting at your uniform."

She twisted free of him and began running toward the Navajo position. Grayson stood slackly for a moment, mindful of Carson's orders to turn back when the girl had been put in contact with the Indians, but suffering an agony of indecision. The distance between him and Micaela lengthened. She began to shout in the Navajo tongue. Watching her, aware that the Indians probably would in all certainty shoot at his uniform if he approached, Grayson succeeded in convincing himself it was wisest to turn back — that Micaela would fare best alone — that a soldier's first duty was to obey his orders — that a junior officer must let responsibility for difficult decisions rest with his superiors. But before he could turn, the ambush in the broken rock toward which Micaela was running exploded with all the violence of the two previous points of Navajo resistance farther down the canyon.

A musket slug, sawing an erratic, noisy

path through the air, struck Grayson a devastating blow on the thigh and spilled him violently to the ground. More lead sang angrily over his head. He rolled over, spitting sand from his mouth, and came to his knees. Sand was in his eyes. He scrubbed it frantically away. Micaela was down on her face, motionless, forty yards away.

He surged to his feet. Behind him, seemingly half the world away, he heard the startled, brassy yelping of bugles as the command signaled formation and charged to support the girl who had tried to carry a truce to the Indians. Grayson knew it would be too late — that it was already too late. He swore violently until he was aware the tearing in his throat was a sob and not profanity.

Beyond Micaela, far beyond — beyond even the Navajo position — a horseman was riding hard down the canyon. He was trailed by another rider, perhaps a quarter of a mile behind him. A couple of Indians, apparently, moving down to support their ambush party.

These things and the smoke above the Navajo position and the heat of the sun were flashing impressions. What was indelibly engraved on his mind was the prone figure of Micaela, face down and motionless on the sand. Grayson tried to run. His wounded leg buckled and he fell. He clawed again to his feet and this time achieved a drunken, staggering progress.

The distance to the girl's body seemed interminable. And the Navajo guns were a roaring thunder. Death was in the air about him, but he was unaware of it. Hope lifted in him when he saw Micaela stir and begin to rise just as he reached her. He flung down in a long, awkward dive, twisting frantically so that his body shielded her, and he forced her roughly back down. But he was too late. The Indians, apparently concentrating their fire on him in the belief the girl was already dead, had discovered she was yet alive. It was either that or the belief both Micaela and himself were helpless and could be reached for some extra savagery before the troop came up. At any rate, thirty or forty of them broke from cover and came racing across the sand.

Raising his head to watch the charging Navajo, Grayson saw the nearest of the two horsemen pounding down the canyon was much closer now. The rider veered as though to race the Indians to their victims. Micaela, sensing Grayson's interest, also lifted her face from the sand. Somehow identity of the horseman was almost instantaneous with her.

"Rick!" she breathed. "Rick!"

Grayson guessed his eyes were still gravelly. He took her word the foremost of the two riders was Lindquist. And it was apparent the mountain man, mounted as he was, would beat the Indians. Grayson twisted around a little to be out of Lindquist's way as he rode up. He twisted around and drew his gun to give Rick as much cover as he could from the front ranks of the leaping Indians. Anything to give Lindquist time enough to get the wounded Micaela up with him onto his horse.

It was funny, it not making much difference whether this rider was Lindquist or the devil or a guardian angel. His arrival got Micaela out of this. If she wasn't too badly hurt, she'd be all right then. The rest of it didn't make much difference. The force of the bullet blow which had struck Grayson indicated his leg was likely half shot away, and in this country, far from competent surgeons, a man didn't survive a severe thigh wound. Too much blood was always lost. When a man was a soldier, he got shot. Micaela had said something like that. And she had been right. Good old Lindquist, the long-geared old bastard. So he got the girl, after all. If he didn't, it wasn't Steve Grayson's fault. That was for sure. Grayson felt pretty good. He'd get a tear out of Micaela for a long time after this; maybe even out of Rick Lindquist — maybe even out of Carson. Glory, they said when a man took his commission. This was what they were talking about.

The first of the two riders came on until even Grayson was sure of his identity. A lean, long man riding like Satan with a fire on his tail. A figure of a man, whether he was a traitor or not. Something beautiful to behold, the way he pounded across the sand.

Then suddenly Lindquist had shot on past without pulling up, without a pause or an attempt to pick up the wounded girl crouching with Grayson. Not even giving them a glance that Grayson could see. Just hammering on down the canyon. And all there was left were the charging Navajo and the second rider, now close enough to the Indians to be shouting at them in their own language. As he shouted, this second rider reined in an arc as though joining the first of the Indians in their race toward Grayson and Micaela. Grayson saw the rider was a Navajo himself, and he made a fine, high target on his horse.

A man got the hell shot out of him, but he died fighting. Grayson carefully raised his gun and sighted it at the Navajo horseman. His shot was set up, the kind a man knew he wouldn't miss. He was bearing unhurried pressure on the trigger and feeling elation beforehand when Micaela seized the gun recklessly by its barrel and destroyed his aim.

"Estevan, no!" she cried. "It's Chief Juanito!"

There couldn't be a better reason for firing off the gun as far as Grayson was concerned. He struggled to free the weapon, Micaela clung desperately to it.

"Estevan, look! Look, please!"

Micaela rose to her knees. Grayson did clumsily likewise. The Indian on the horse had cut in front of the charging Navajo and pivoted to face them. They had halted. The balance of their ambush force was filing out of the rocks in which they had holed up, their guns lowered. There was no gun sound in the canyon. Grayson twisted awkwardly around. Fifty yards from Micaela and himself, Captain Pfieffer and Captain Carey had drawn up their hastily mounted troopers in almost parade-ground trim. In front of them Colonel Carson and Eric Lindquist, dismounted, were advancing toward the girl and himself. It was suddenly so quiet he could hear the sand crunching beneath their boots.

Grayson blinked. Deflation shook him. He was all filled up with wryness and bitterness — and about as much anger as he could contain. He had made as much sacrifice as a man could contrive. Apparently it had been useless. As useless as Micaela's foolhardy attempt to reach Juanito through the Navajo ambush.

"Skirmish Number Three," he said to himself, savagely mocking a report someone would presently have to make to Carson. "Casualties, two . . ."

Micaela must have heard the words. She glanced quickly at him and saw for the first time the sand-caked blood on his uniform.

"Estevan, you're hurt!"

"A scratch," he lied.

"You — you should have — how do you say it? — you should have hit the dirt when the shooting started, Estevan. The Navajo taught me to do that a long time ago."

Her voice was strong. Micaela was smiling a little, as though in encouragement to him. Grayson blinked at her.

"Then you're not — you're not —" He

broke off, his question answered. Micaela had come quickly to her feet. She ran out to meet Carson and Rick Lindquist. And the freedom of her movements betrayed no sign of injury.

Grayson swore softly and made a noble effort to rise also. To his surprise, he managed to do this. And when he tried to take a step, he found he could walk with reasonable comfort. In addition, there was less blood on his uniform than he had imagined. Very little, in fact. He remembered the flat, sawing sound of the musket ball which had struck him, a sound betraying a splattered shape and low velocity, had he thought of it. Just the same, he had a remarkable constitution. Bullets bounced off him. It had happened twice now. He might live forever. A bleak enough prospect, unless he could get Micaela to find a little time to hear him out.

A soldier had to make love in the most unreasonable places and against the most exasperating odds. He couldn't even trust his own reactions. Life got to be so damned uncertain. He swore again and, limping slightly, crossed to where she had stopped with Lindquist and the colonel, facing the approaching chief of the Navajo and a delegation of his men. When

Grayson came up beside her, Micaela did not turn her head. Juanito of the Navajo had begun to speak, and she was listening to him.

Beyond the parley the balance of the Navajo ambush was grouped in the open, no longer a hostile party. Others, apparently from more defense positions farther up the canyon, were moving down to join them. Grayson grudgingly recognized the hopefulness which seemed to have replaced their hostility. In the opposite direction were his own comrades at arms, at ease in their saddles and obviously relieved to be sitting motionless in the sun rather than riding into enemy bullets. Even Captain Pfieffer seemed content. It looked like the end of what could have been a first-class war. Grayson, who in the beginning had not been overjoyed at the prospect of battle, resented this cessation of hostilities. He felt like fighting somebody tooth and nail about now and he wasn't a bit particular whom, so long as he could get on with it.

It was midafternoon before the parley on the floor of the canyon broke up. Lindquist worked hard and impatiently throughout its interminable length. Carson had to find something about which to be stubborn in order to counteract the stubbornness of the Navajo. He chose to refuse to countermand his original orders to the Utes up the canyon until Chief Juanito and the Navajo Council came to agreement on his basic terms. As a result, the prolonged bickering had chafed, the burden being made unbearable by the knowledge that at any time a tactical error on the part of the Navajo warriors guarding the slowly retreating nation far up-canyon might put the whole shebang at the mercy of the Utes. And having lost men the night before, the Utes would show no mercy. Should Ute and Navajo really tangle far up-canyon, peace here would be impossible.

Finally Carson relented. He sent Captain Pfieffer with a detachment and a couple of old men of the Navajo Council up de Chelly to order the Utes off and escort the Navajo caravan back down the canyon. This gesture happily settled Juanito's doubts as to the honesty of the only offer Carson could make to him, and the chief agreed to the necessary surrender. It was no gleeful occasion, but it solved what had been heretofore the unsolvable.

Juanito pulled out to face his people

with the agreement their chief and the Council had made with the *yanqui* soldiers. Young Grayson, limping, avoiding Lindquist with unnecessarily bitter aversion, and in a very foul mood for making love, took Micaela Castaneda across the canyon to a shady spot beneath some cottonwoods, where they sat a little apart in earnest talk. Old Castaneda and Carson and Lindquist found themselves alone. Castaneda was having difficulty sharing Chief Juanito's eventual faith in the promises Carson had made to him.

"As I understand the *coronel*," the old man said carefully, "he is personally guaranteeing the return of the Navajo from Bosque Redondo after a reasonable time?"

"I couldn't guarantee anything," Carson regretted. "That's out of my hands completely. But I've agreed to use whatever influence I have to get Chief Juanito's people back here as quickly as possible. It is my belief they should not be removed from here. It has always been. But some of them have been guilty of raiding ranches off and on, and a number of them were unquestionably involved in the Taos rebellion. Some punishment is due, I suppose. All I promise is to try to have it made as light as possible."

"You have enough influence to do this?" Castaneda inquired anxiously.

Lindquist rolled over on his stomach to face the old man.

"After this campaign — talking the biggest Indian tribe in the country into surrendering to the tiny force he has here, Kit Carson will own the government west of the Missouri and south of the Platte," he said.

Carson shook his head. "I'll agree this campaign isn't going to hurt me any at all, thanks to you, Rick. But it isn't that. It's what I can honestly put in my reports, to be verified by the Regular Army officers under me here. Pfieffer, Carey, and Grayson."

"I wouldn't think reports of engagements with hostile Navajo would be a good influence for the Navajo with your government," Castaneda protested.

"No?" Carson asked. "Look at this. At any time after Captain Pfieffer's arrival here with Lindquist, the Navajo were strong enough to have wiped out my entire command in a stroke. Nevertheless, although they knew our purpose, they made no resistance to us until we entered their canyons. They fought defensively then — even today. Captain Pfieffer's detachment escaped last night at cost of his arms alone

307

when he could have lost every man in his company. Lindquist here managed that, trying to save the Navajo from me. I wanted them saved. That's why I did my level best to force him to go over to them."

"You can quit boasting, Kit," Lindquist growled at him. "It was a damned dirty trick!"

"Still the Navajo have to march to Bosque Redondo — still they have to make the Long Walk." Castaneda was persistent. Carson nodded.

"They'll have to stay at Bosque Redondo until these arguments work for them. But how long is Washington going to support seven or eight or ten thousand Indians who proved they want to be peaceable and who can support themselves on their own lands?"

This seemed to make a great deal of sense to Castaneda. He looked out across the sandy floor of the canyon. His daughter and Steve Grayson were coming back from the cottonwoods. They didn't seem to be in any hurry, but Lindquist noted with satisfaction that they weren't holding hands, either. They moved up to the group and joined it. Carson grinned maliciously across at Grayson.

"Do we have to locate an extra horse and

rig up a sidesaddle for the ride back to Santa Fe, son?"

Grayson scowled blackly. He drew a sharp line in the sand with one finger.

"She won't give me an answer, sir."

"No?" Carson seemed most sympathetic. "Unreasonable of her, isn't it? She shoots you. Next she helps Lindquist slip away from you at gunpoint. Then she gets you shot by the Navajo. And then no satisfaction. That's a woman for you!"

Both Micaela and her father, catching the humor dancing in Carson's eyes, laughed. Grayson did not. He was dead serious and he obviously did not think Carson was an amusing man. Castaneda asked his daughter something in a Spanish too swift for Lindquist to follow. She answered shortly in the same manner. Carson turned to the old man.

"Seems I recollect promising to put you back on your *estancia* when we were done with the Navajo. I better do something about that."

Castaneda shook his head.

"I am too old to build much again," he said without rancor. "Never in the big canyon, anyway. De Chelly is for the Navajo when they come back. Always it should be for them. For me, perhaps one of the side canyons. There are many fine places here for stock. But it depends upon my daughter, señor. The lieutenant is waiting for her answer. I'm afraid I wait for it also."

"Guess that brings us around to you, then, Rick," Carson said lightly.

"I'll get along," Lindquist told him stiffly.

"Sure," Carson agreed. "You're a getting-along kind. But you've got to get this straight. You got to know there wasn't anything personal in this. You got to understand that as far as you were concerned I was just using the best tool I could lay hands on in a hurry for the job I had to do."

Lindquist stretched his long frame and eyed the chief of scouts.

"You know, Kit, every now and then you get a little too big for your britches. No use you taking all the credit. I didn't do anything because I was tricked into it. . . ."

"Except ride past Micaela, there," Carson reminded him dryly, "when you and everybody else thought she'd been hit by Navajo fire and the Indians were going to get to her to finish her off."

"Yeah, except that," Lindquist agreed. "I'd already made your promises to Juanito for you, but your blasted soldiers and this lower Navajo bunch were headed straight toward each other's throats, bent on making a liar out of me. I had to stop you and hope to hell Juanito could stop his Indians before all hell broke loose. There wasn't time for anything else. And Grayson was with Micaela. I figured he could hold the Navajo off till I doubled back."

"I know, Rick," Carson agreed with sudden earnestness. "It was a devil of a decision. I'm in your debt. But to give the Navajo the best cards we can, I've got to report facts, all the way through."

"And one of those facts is that I deserted to the enemy."

"Afraid it is, Rick. I'm afraid you're done scouting for the Army. And if you ever get back too far east, you may run into real trouble because of Army warrants. I was thinking, if you'd sort of headquarter at my post at Taos —"

"Thanks, Kit, but the way I feel, even Taos is too far east for me. Matter of fact, I reckon I'm about as far east as I'm ever going again, right now — and as far west, too."

Micaela looked up sharply at this, her attention withdrawing from Grayson's understandably sullen features for the first time. She rose slowly, looking at Lindquist so intently that he fell to wondering uncomfortably if his old buckskins were finally coming apart at the seams. He brushed his hands awkwardly over them, but they seemed to be all right.

"There's no fur out here, Rick," Carson protested. "No nothing, in fact. And you've got to eat. What you going to do?"

Lindquist drew a long breath. It was a hard thing for him to step right out in the open and open up his chest and let a lot of curious eyes see what was at work in the middle of him. But he guessed there were times when a man had to do the hard thing. There was no point in carrying a gun around a lifetime just because he liked the looks of it, afraid to fire it off for fear the barrel would turn out no good and so have to be thrown away. There was only one way to find out whether it was a shooting iron or whether it wasn't.

"I figured I might look into some of these stock canyons Señor Castaneda was talking about," he said. "Maybe pick one that suited me and build a place. Don't know. Guess I'm about in a boat with Steve and Señor Castaneda. Sort of depends on what kind of an answer Micaela gives Steve."

The others looked astonished. Even Carson blinked.

"Well, now, look here, honey," he said briskly, turning to Micaela. "You got us *all* in an uproar. Give the boy his answer!"

Micaela stood completely motionless for a moment. Lindquist thought she relished this instant as she had no other. She was a woman. Finally she moved, but toward Lindquist, much to his surprise, not toward Steve Grayson. She moved up in front of him and looked soberly up into his face, but for all her soberness he could see little devils dancing in her eyes.

She seemed very small, standing there before him. When she reached upward, her hands barely locked at the back of his neck. Lindquist bent, and because this was something very wonderful and very beautiful and might not ever happen again, he kissed her gently. So gently in the beginning and then so fiercely when she clung and did not break away. The others sitting about them on the sand vanished and they were alone in the great red canyon as they had been the night she had first showed him de Chelly.

After a long time Lindquist released her.

She stepped back and ran her tongue imp-ishly over her lips as though critically sa-voring a taste lingering there. She nodded, as though making up her mind with very little effort, and Lindquist realized with the most profound shock of his life that her mind had long been made up — perhaps as long ago as the day she had ridden from timber with Navajo bowmen for protection and demanded the return of her boots from a young cavalry lieutenant and a somewhat weathered man in buckskin.

She turned to Grayson.

"I'm sorry, Estevan," she said. She sounded as though she meant this, but nothing more. "I'm sorry, but the answer is no."

"I'm damned!" Carson breathed, rather more pointedly than necessary. "I'd have lost a bet on that!"

Rick chuckled as Micaela swung back into his arms. The chief of scouts was a de-vious man. Lindquist knew he was lying.

We hope you have enjoyed this Large Print book. Other Thorndike, Wheeler or Chivers Press Large Print books are available at your library or directly from the publishers.

For more information about current and upcoming titles, please call or write, without obligation, to:

Publisher
Thorndike Press
295 Kennedy Memorial Drive
Waterville, ME   04901
Tel. (800) 223-1244

Or visit our Web site at:
www.gale.com/thorndike
www.gale.com/wheeler

OR

Chivers Large Print
published by BBC Audiobooks Ltd
St James House, The Square
Lower Bristol Road
Bath BA2 3SB
England
Tel. +44(0) 800 136919
email: bbcaudiobooks@bbc.co.uk
www.bbcaudiobooks.co.uk

All our Large Print titles are designed for easy reading, and all our books are made to last.